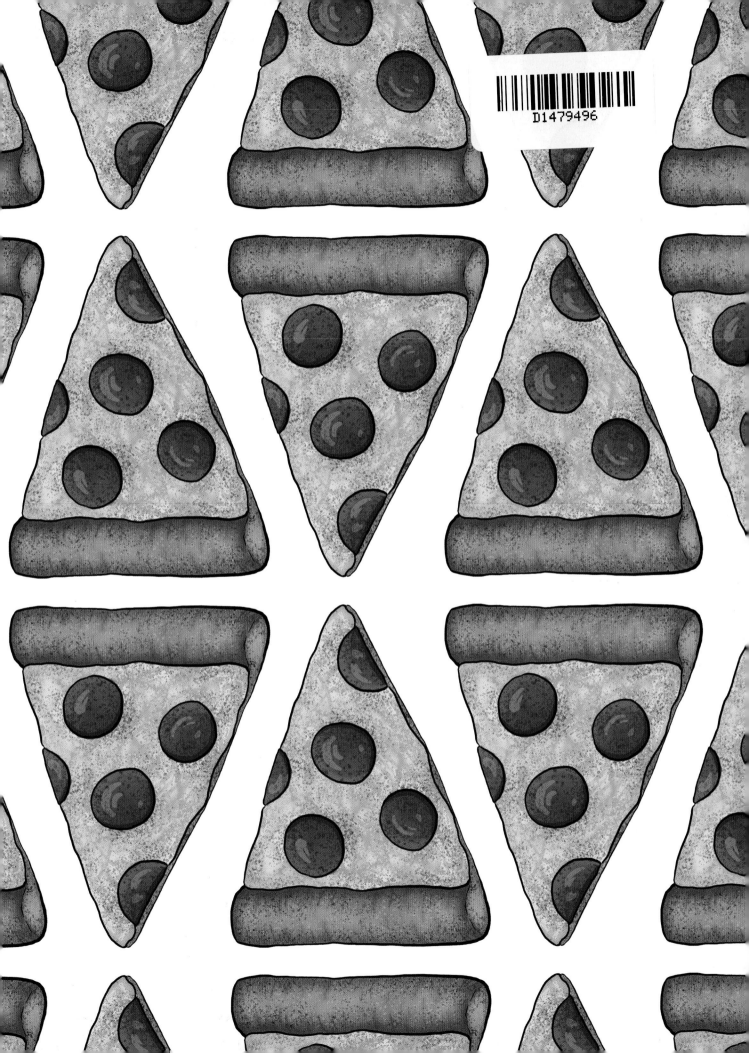

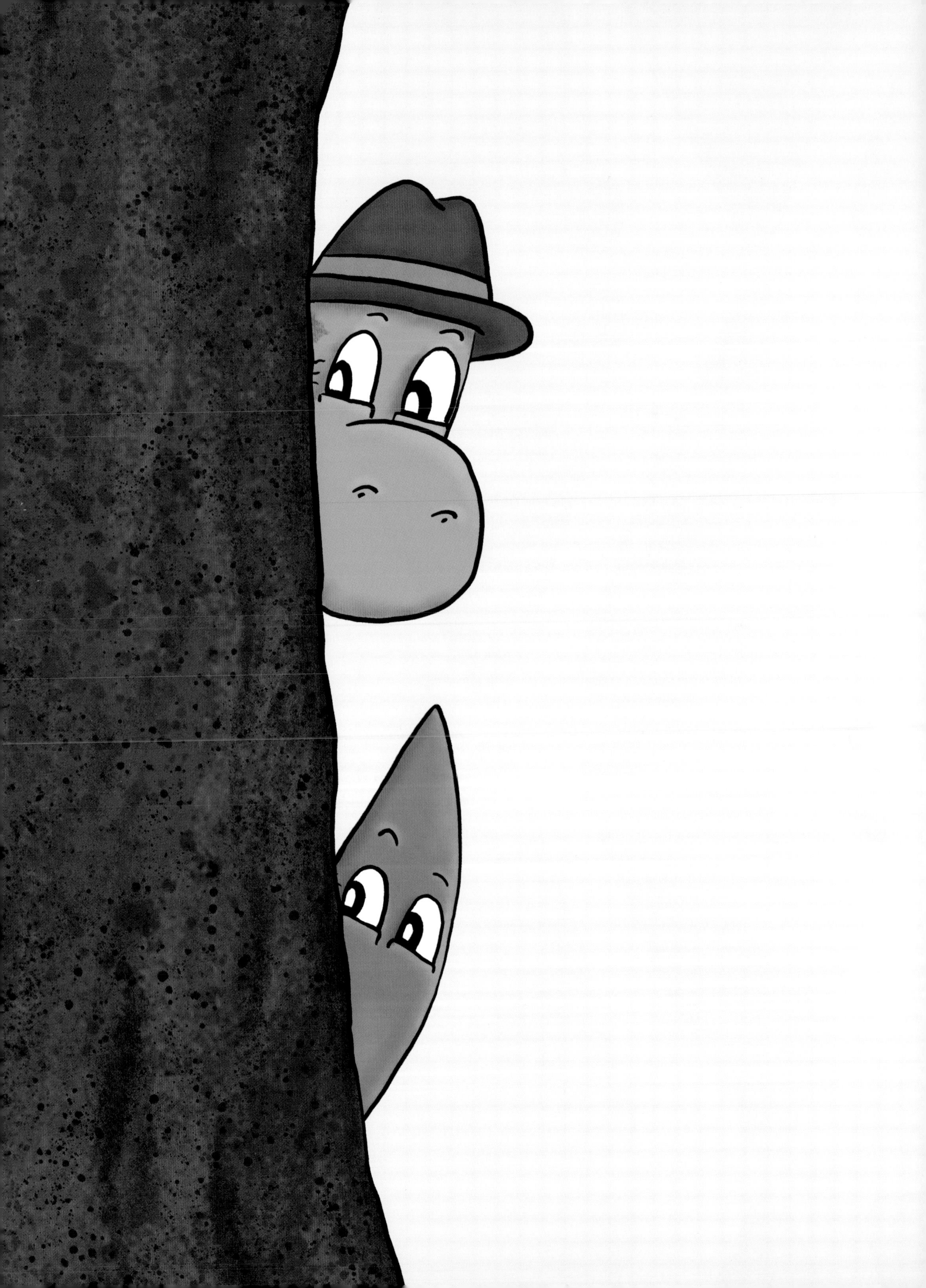

HIDE & GO SEEK-A-SAURUS

BY SHERI ROLOFF

To Joshua + Raen
Pizza rules and
so do you! SHERI ROLOFF

KWiL Publishing
Milwaukee, Wisconsin

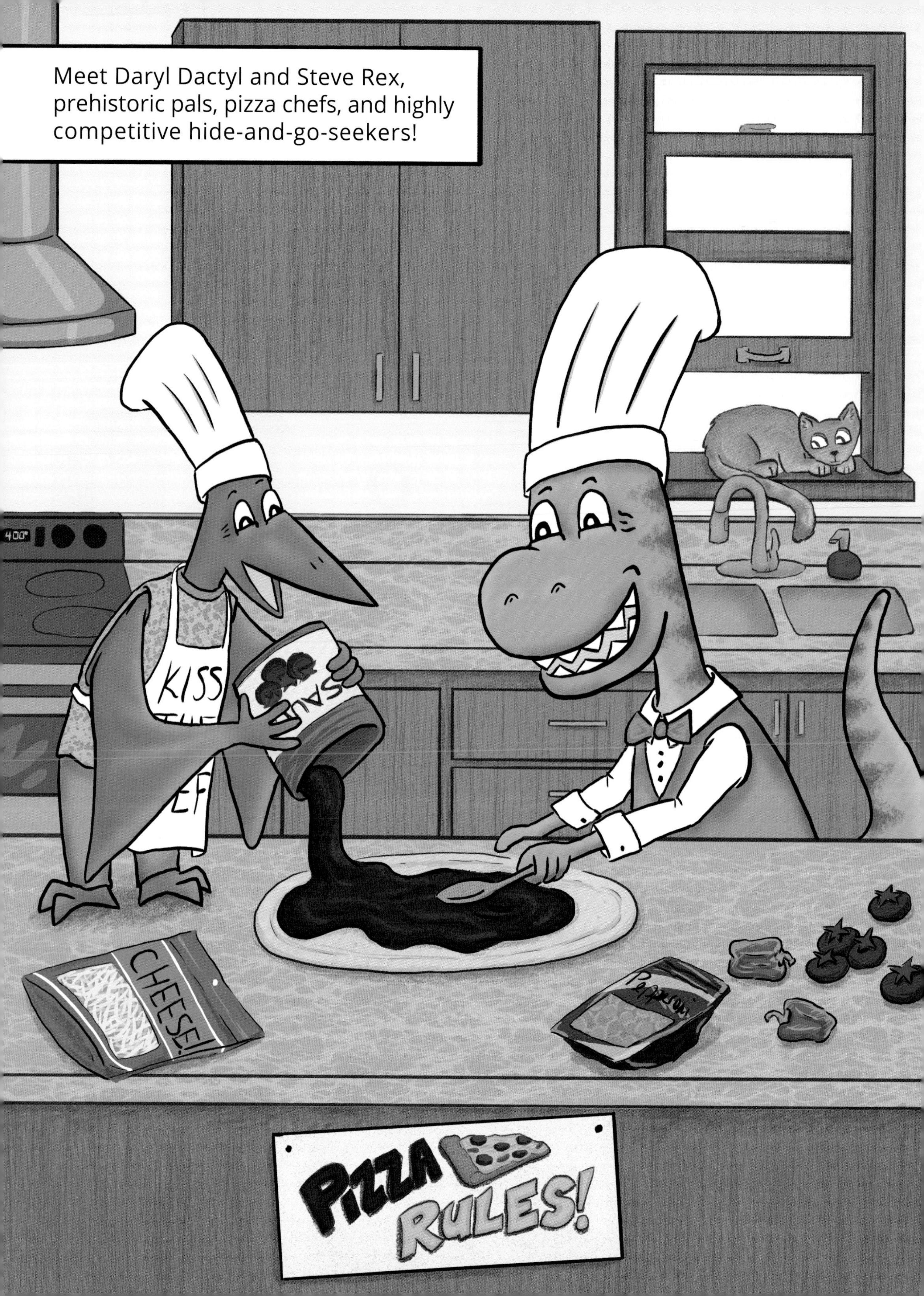
Meet Daryl Dactyl and Steve Rex, prehistoric pals, pizza chefs, and highly competitive hide-and-go-seekers!
KISS
CHEESE!
Pepperoni
PIZZA RULES!

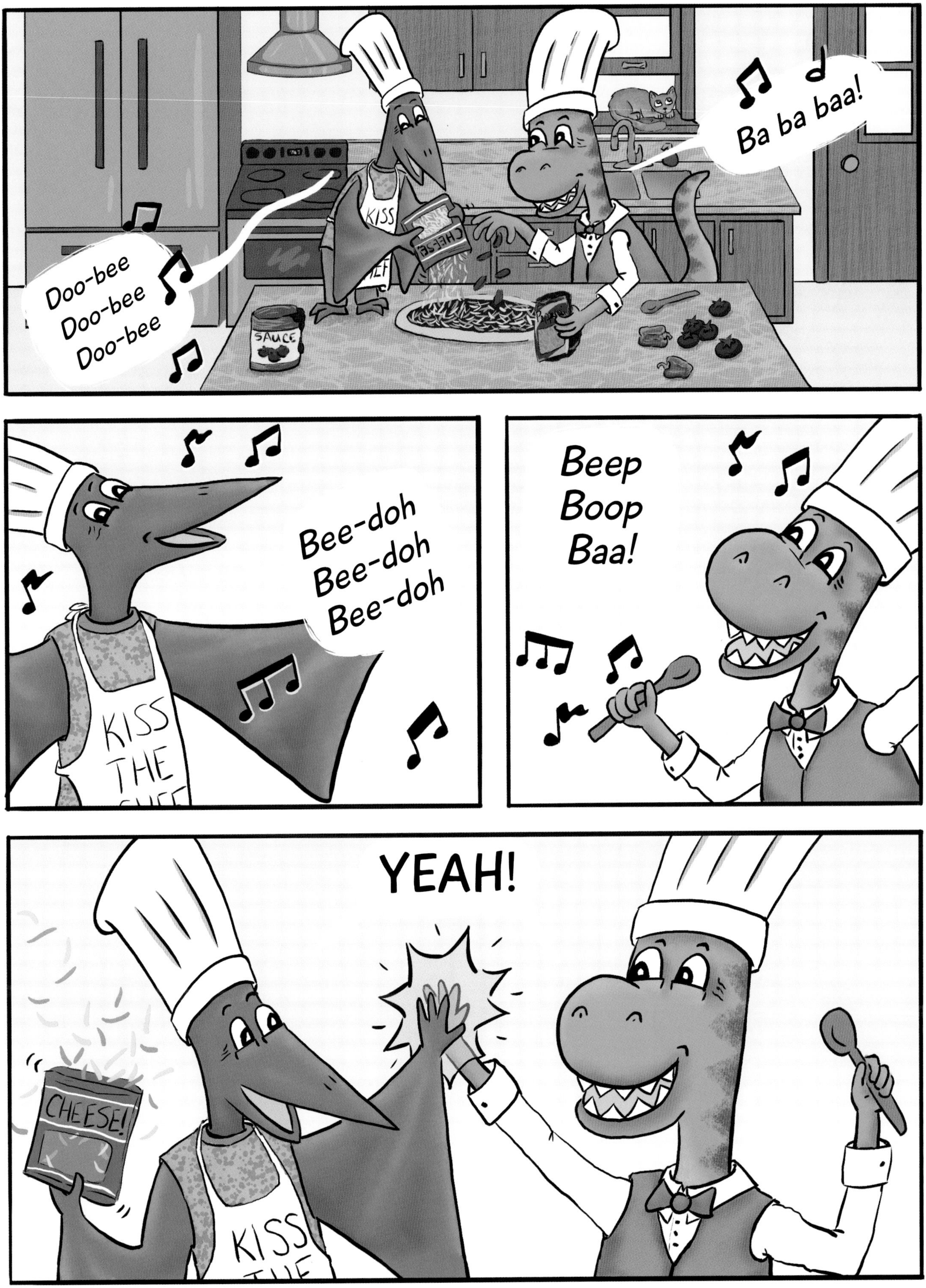
Doo-bee
Doo-bee
Doo-bee
Ba ba baa!
KISS
CHEESE
SAUCE
Bee-doh
Bee-doh
Bee-doh
KISS
THE
Beep
Boop
Baa!
YEAH!
CHEESE!
KISS

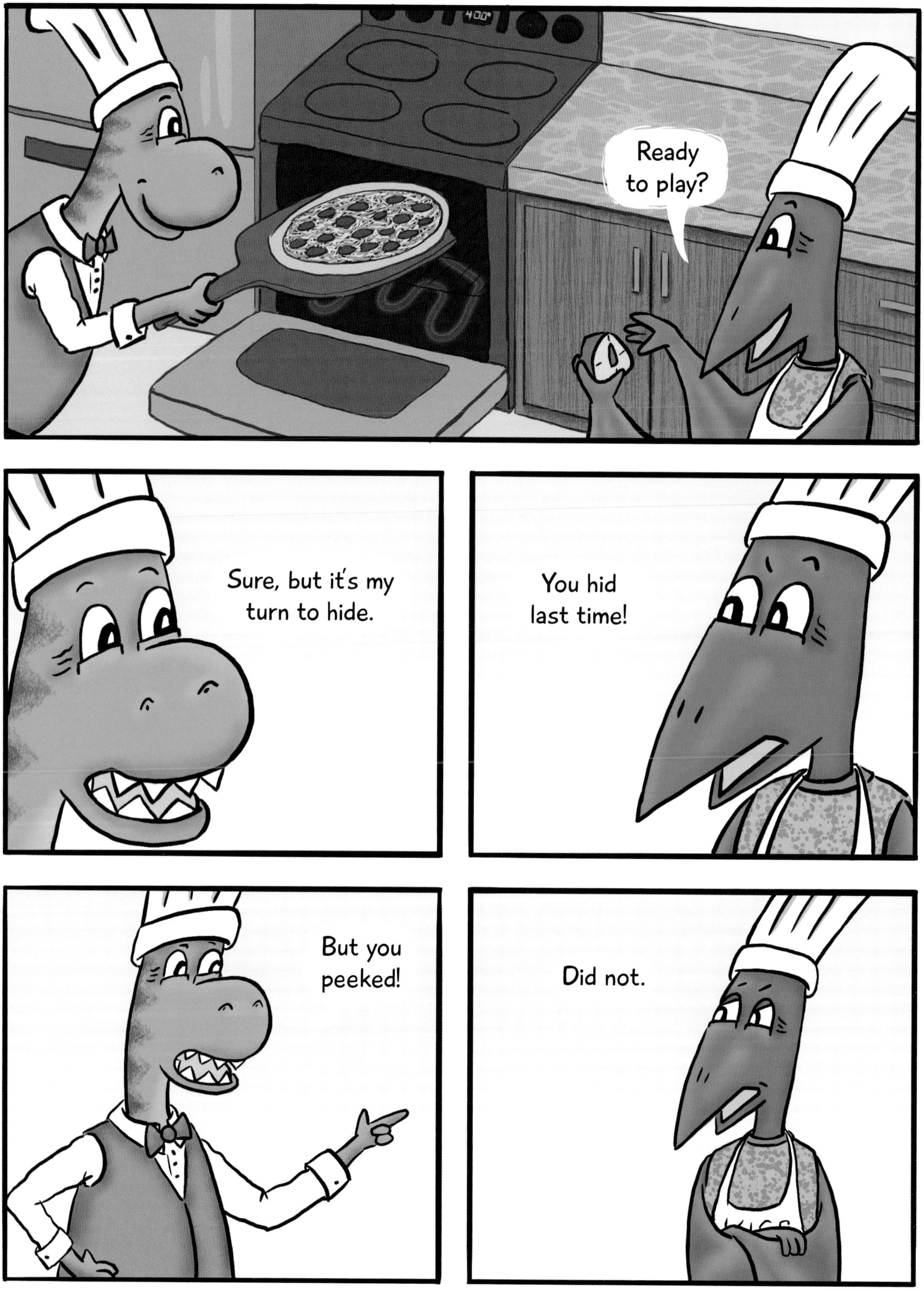
Ready to play?
Sure, but it's my turn to hide.
You hid last time!
But you peeked!
Did not.

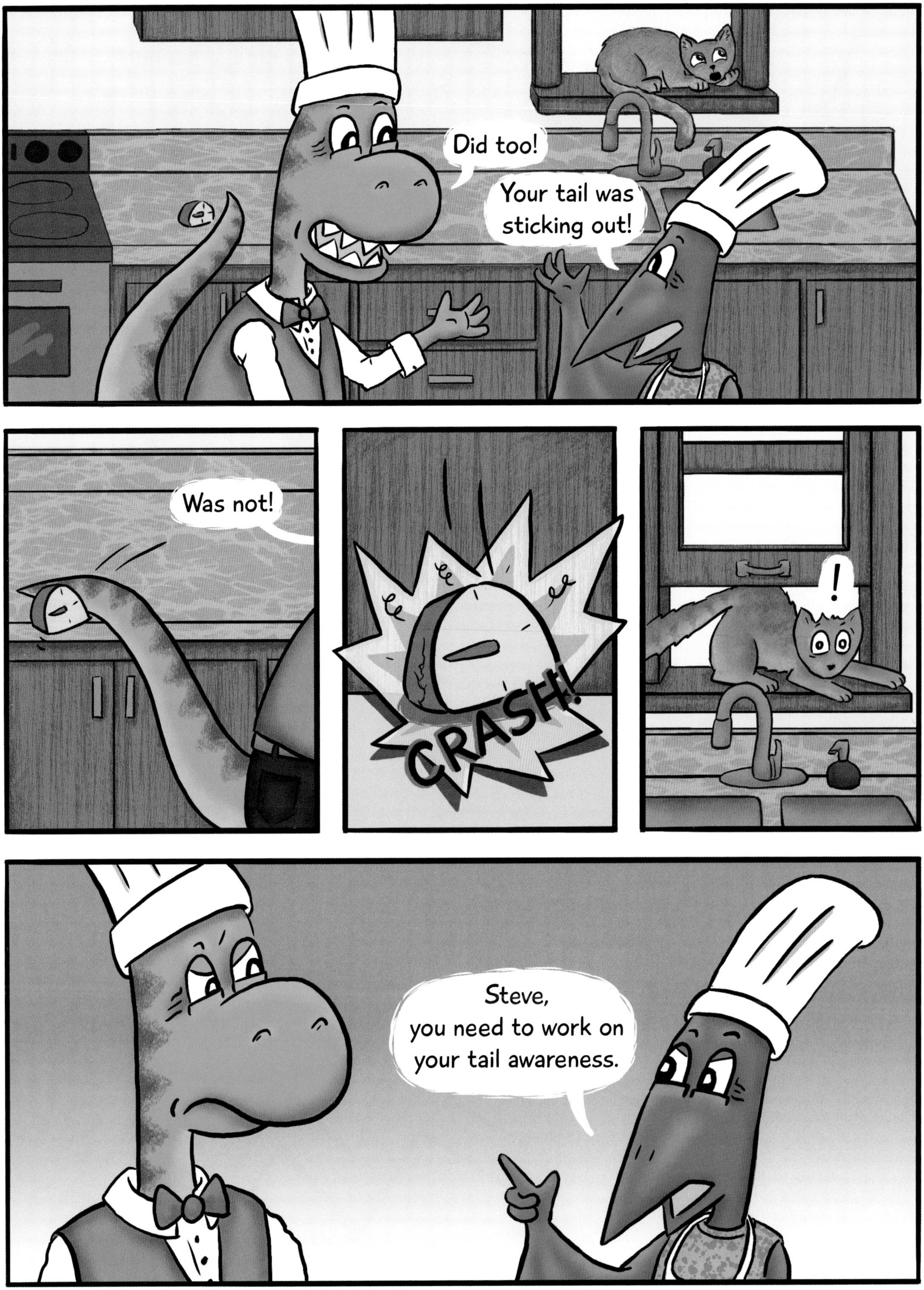
Did too!
Your tail was sticking out!
Was not!
CRASH!
!
Steve, you need to work on your tail awareness.

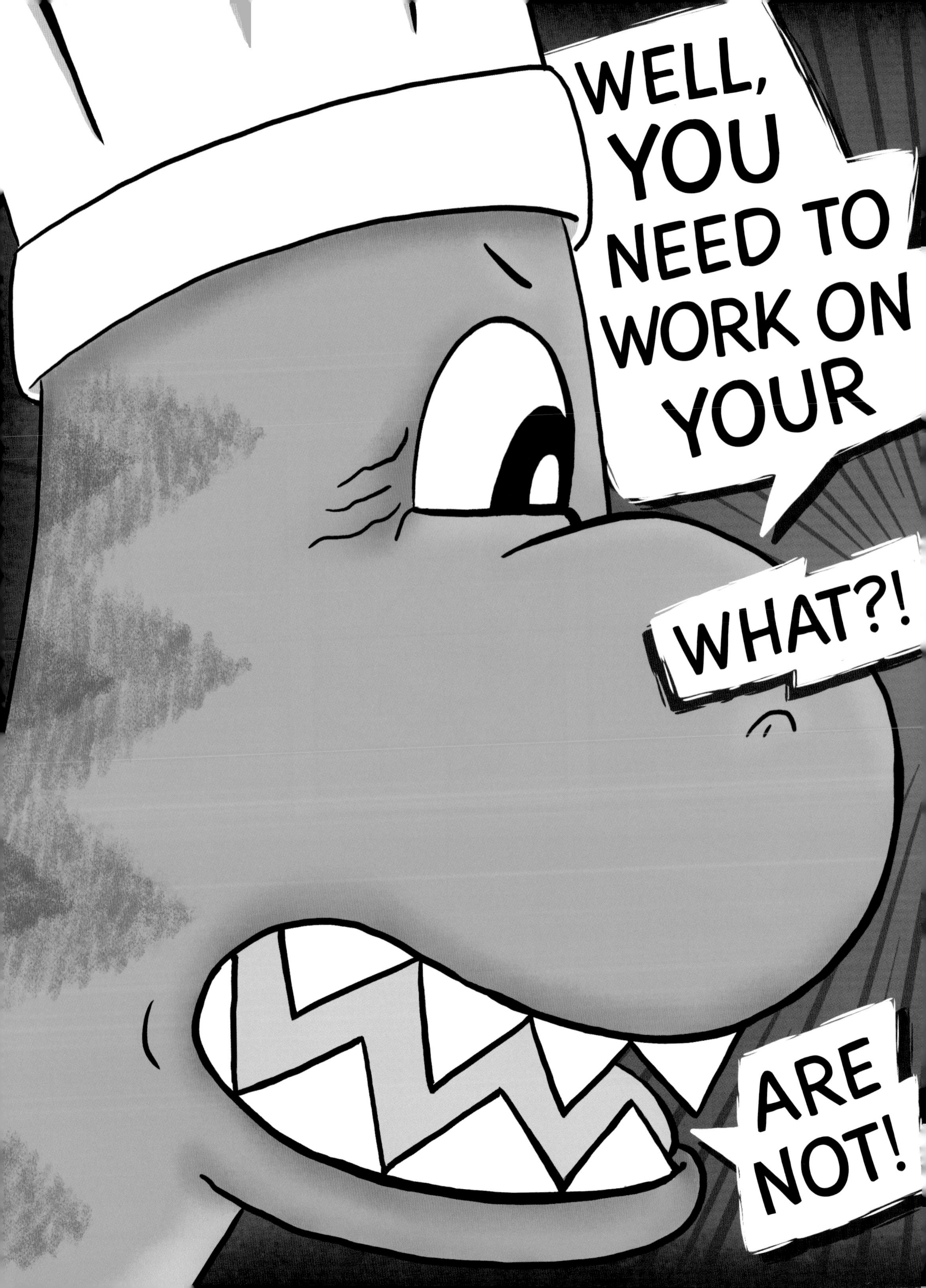
WELL, YOU NEED TO WORK ON YOUR
WHAT?!
ARE NOT!

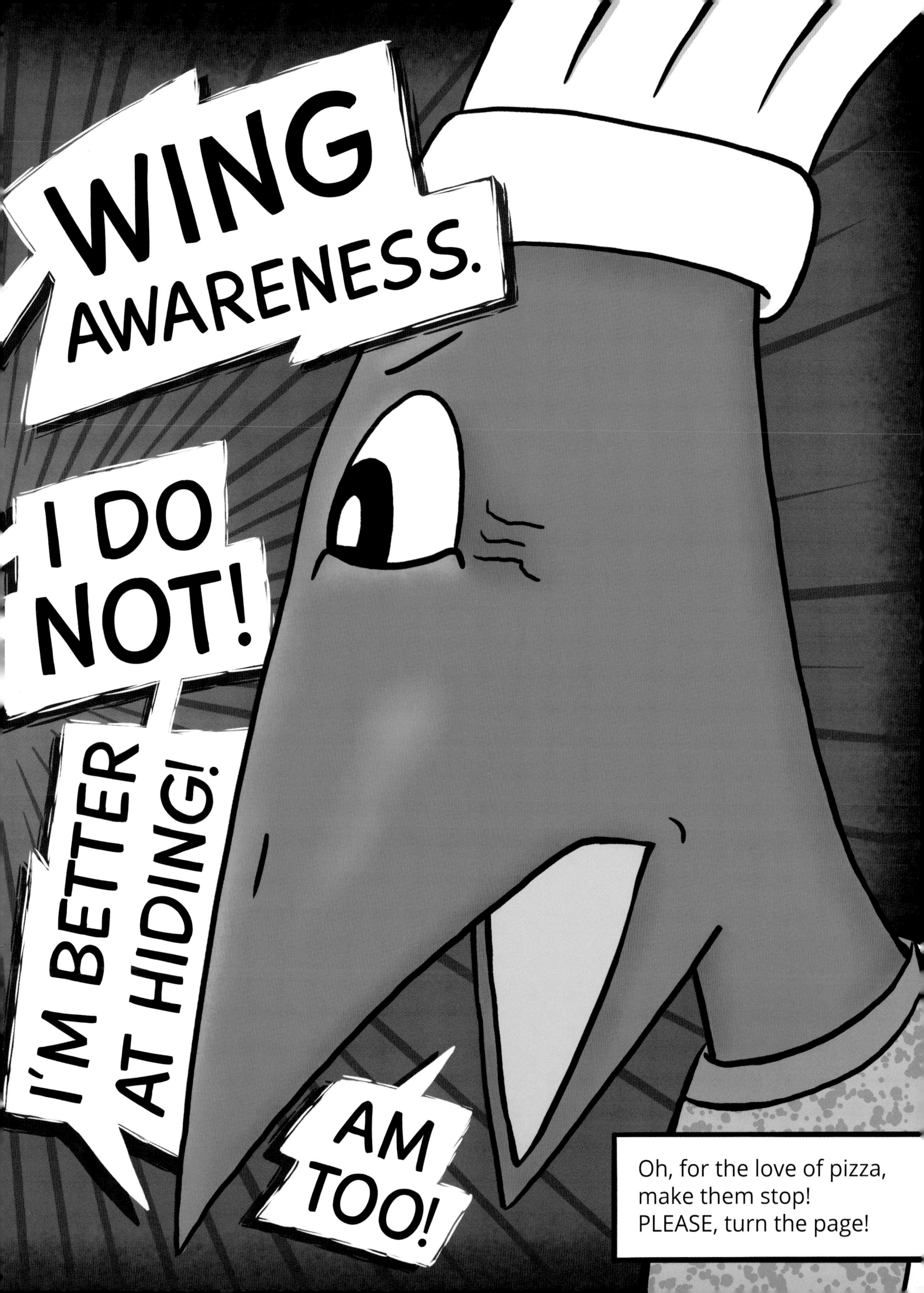
WING AWARENESS.
I DO NOT!
I'M BETTER AT HIDING!
AM TOO!
Oh, for the love of pizza, make them stop! PLEASE, turn the page!

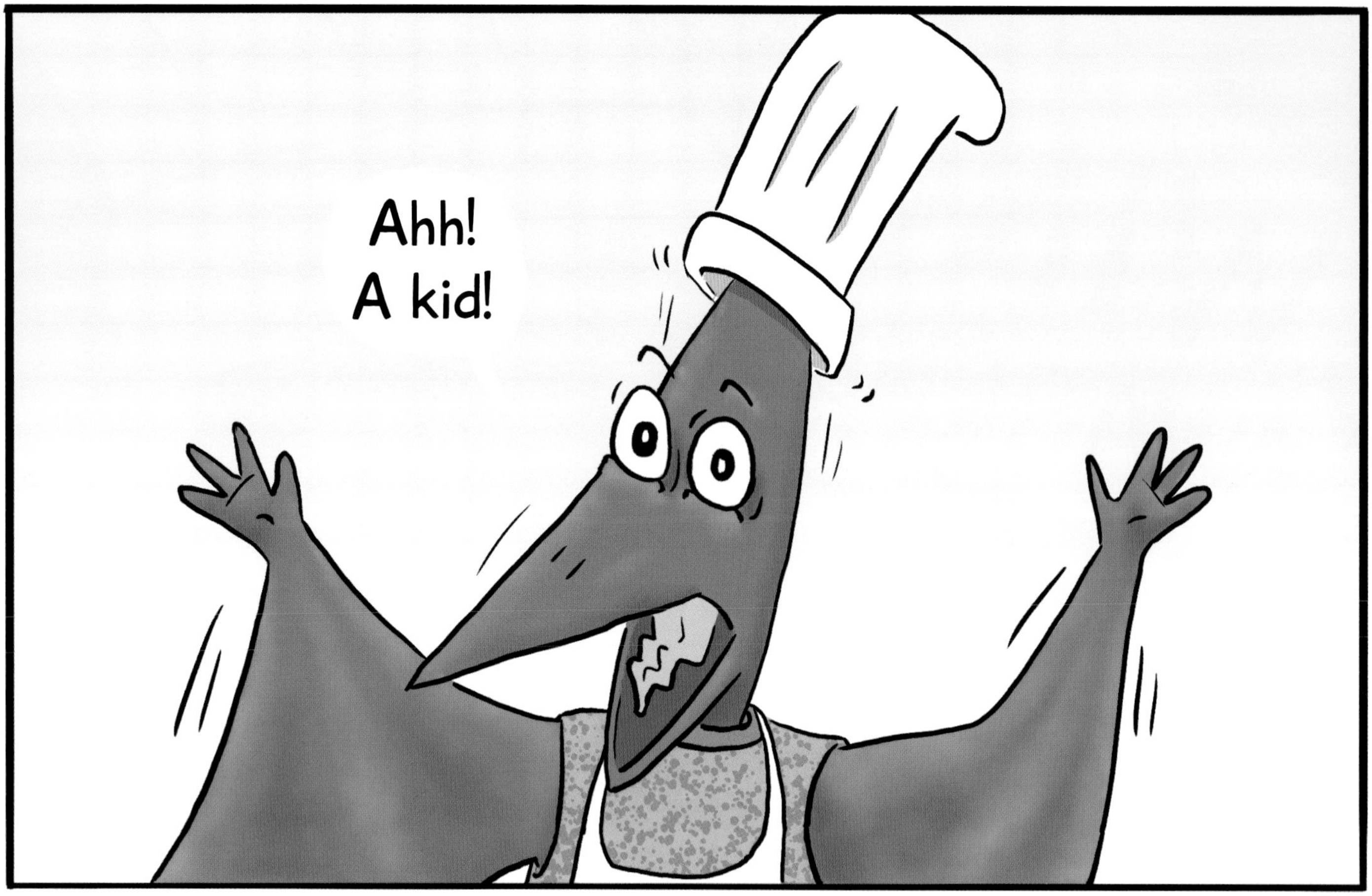
Ahh!
A kid!

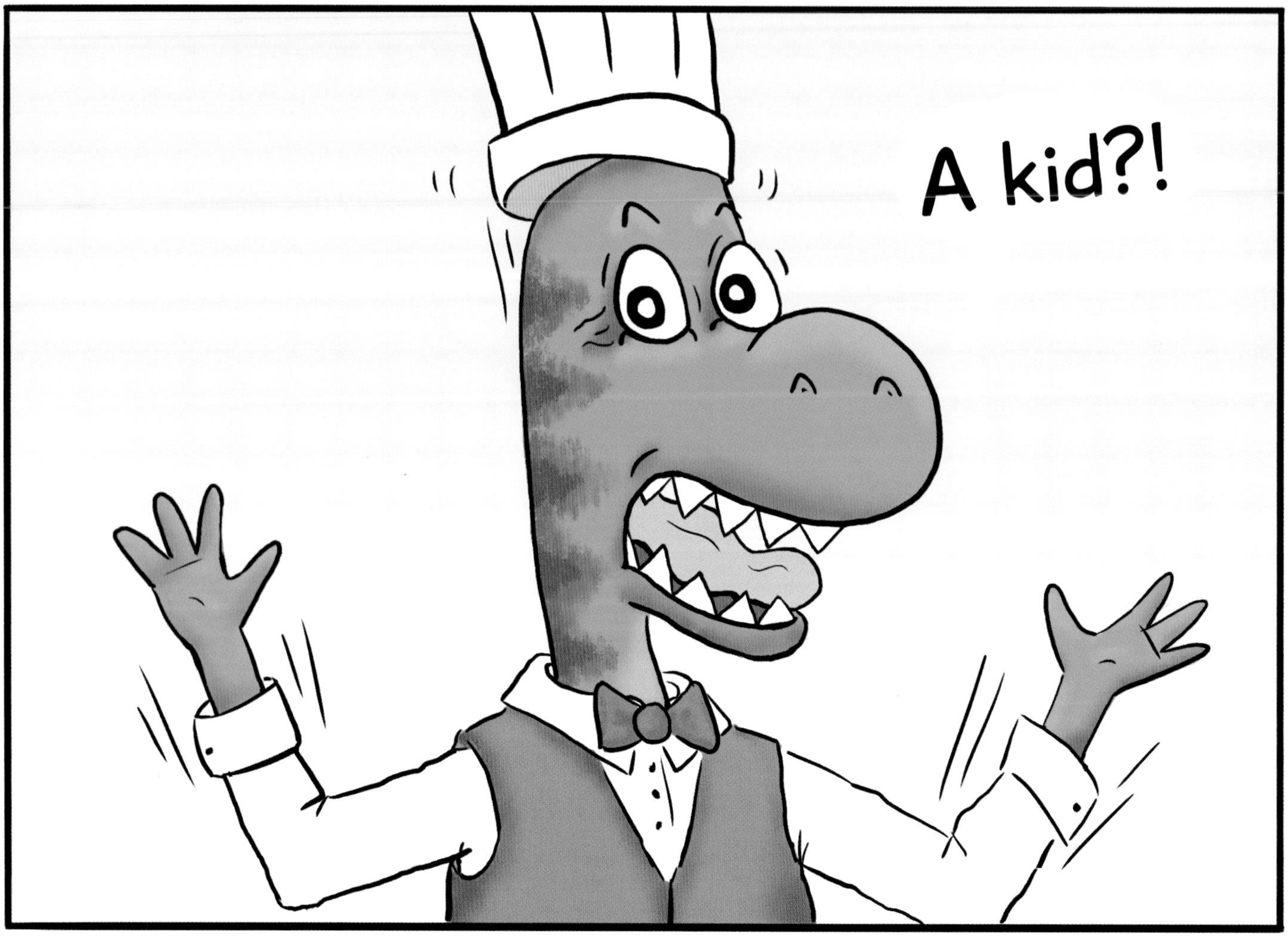
A kid?!

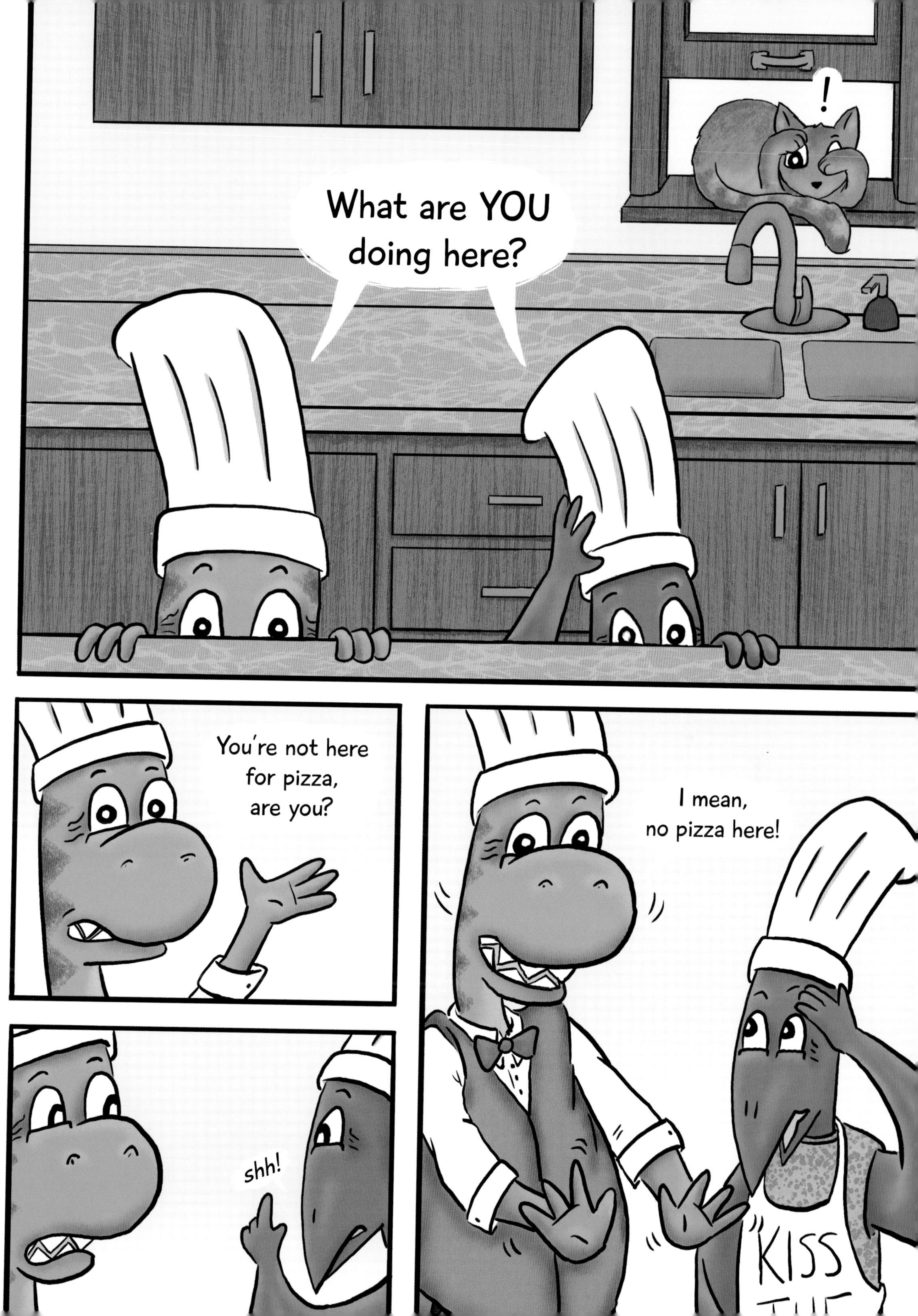
!
What are YOU doing here?
You're not here for pizza, are you?
shh!
I mean, no pizza here!
KISS

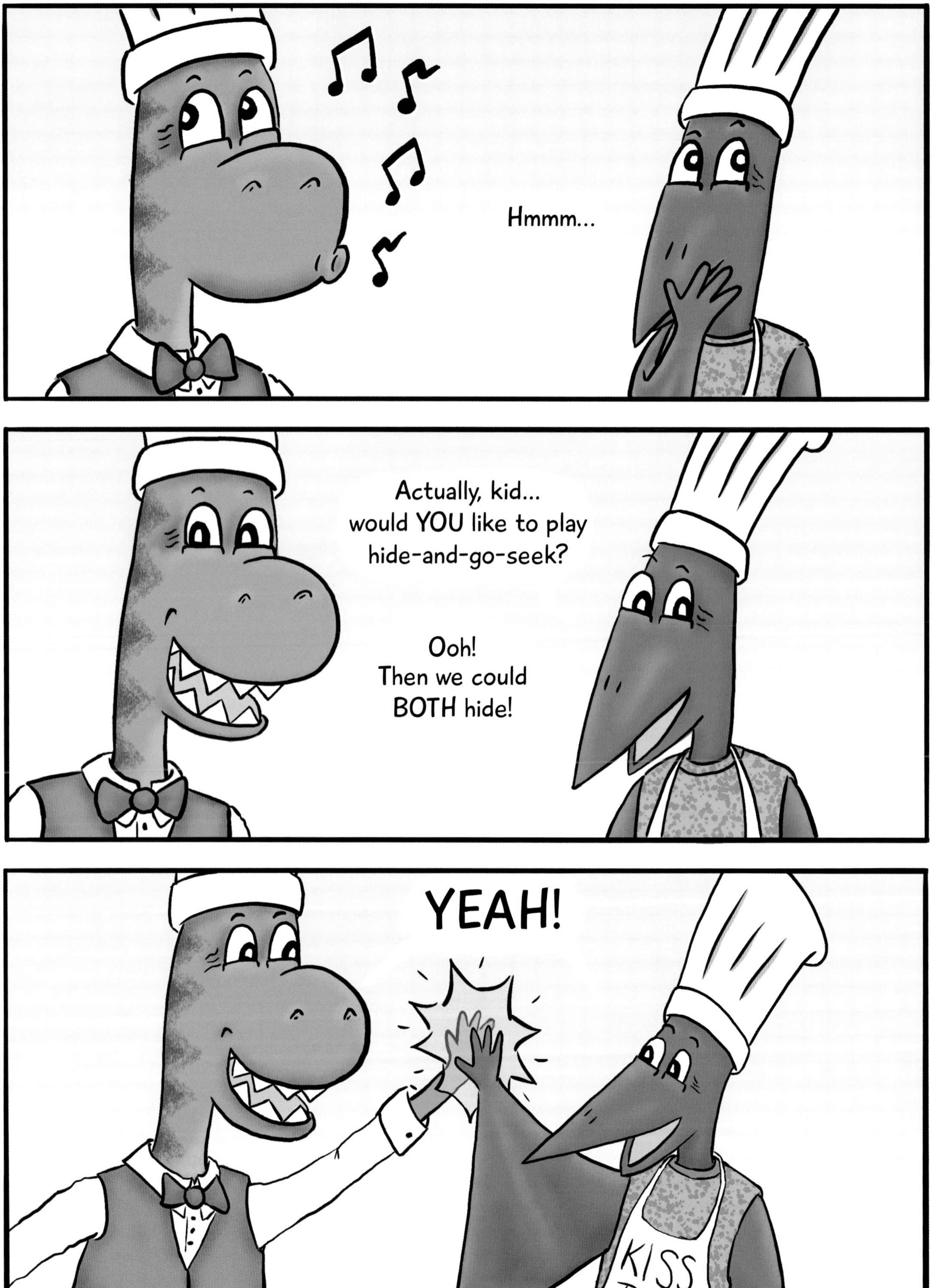
Hmmm...
Actually, kid... would YOU like to play hide-and-go-seek?
Ooh! Then we could BOTH hide!
YEAH!
KISS

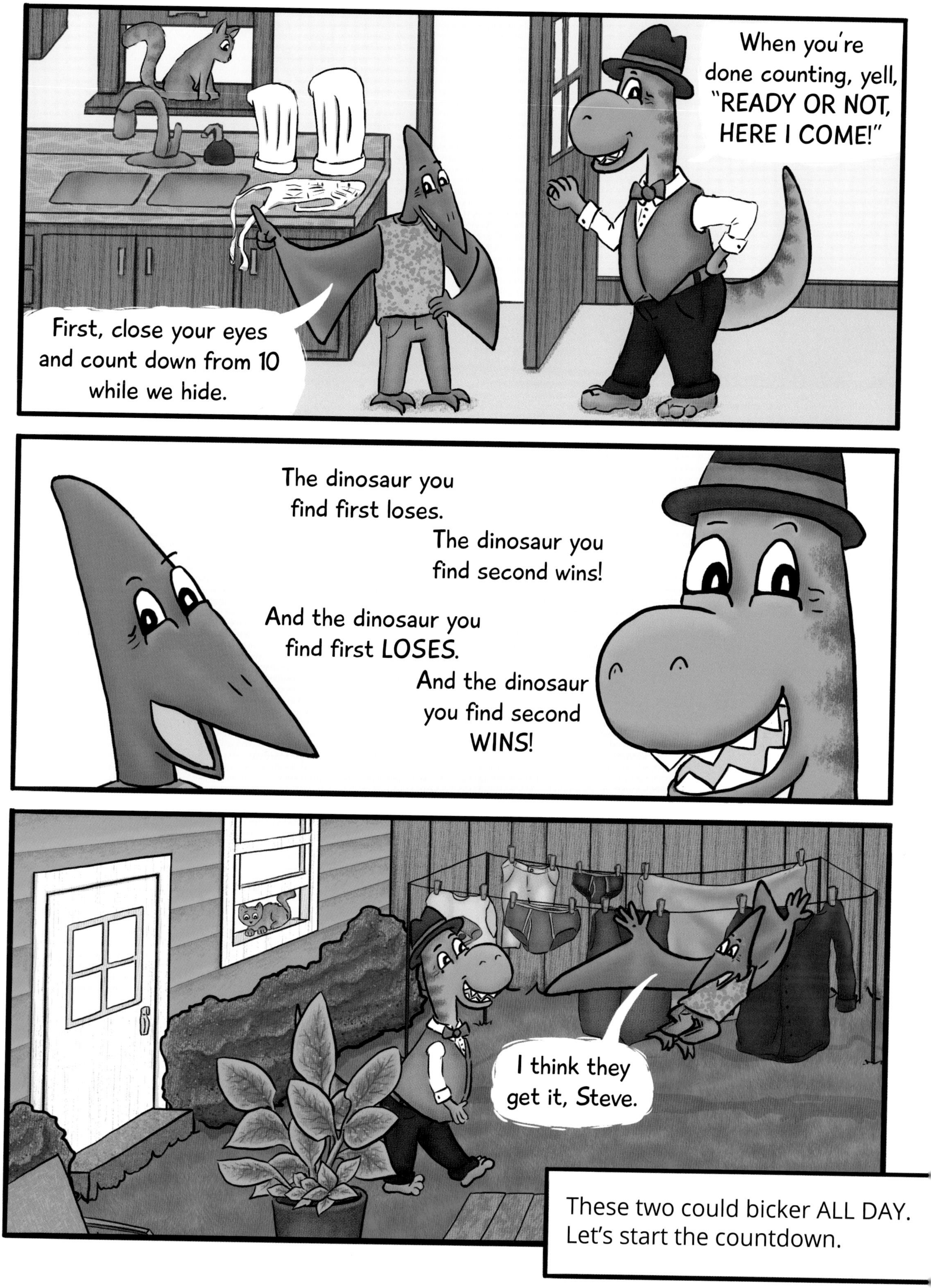
First, close your eyes and count down from 10 while we hide.
When you're done counting, yell, "READY OR NOT, HERE I COME!"
The dinosaur you find first loses.
The dinosaur you find second wins!
And the dinosaur you find first LOSES.
And the dinosaur you find second WINS!
I think they get it, Steve.
These two could bicker ALL DAY. Let's start the countdown.

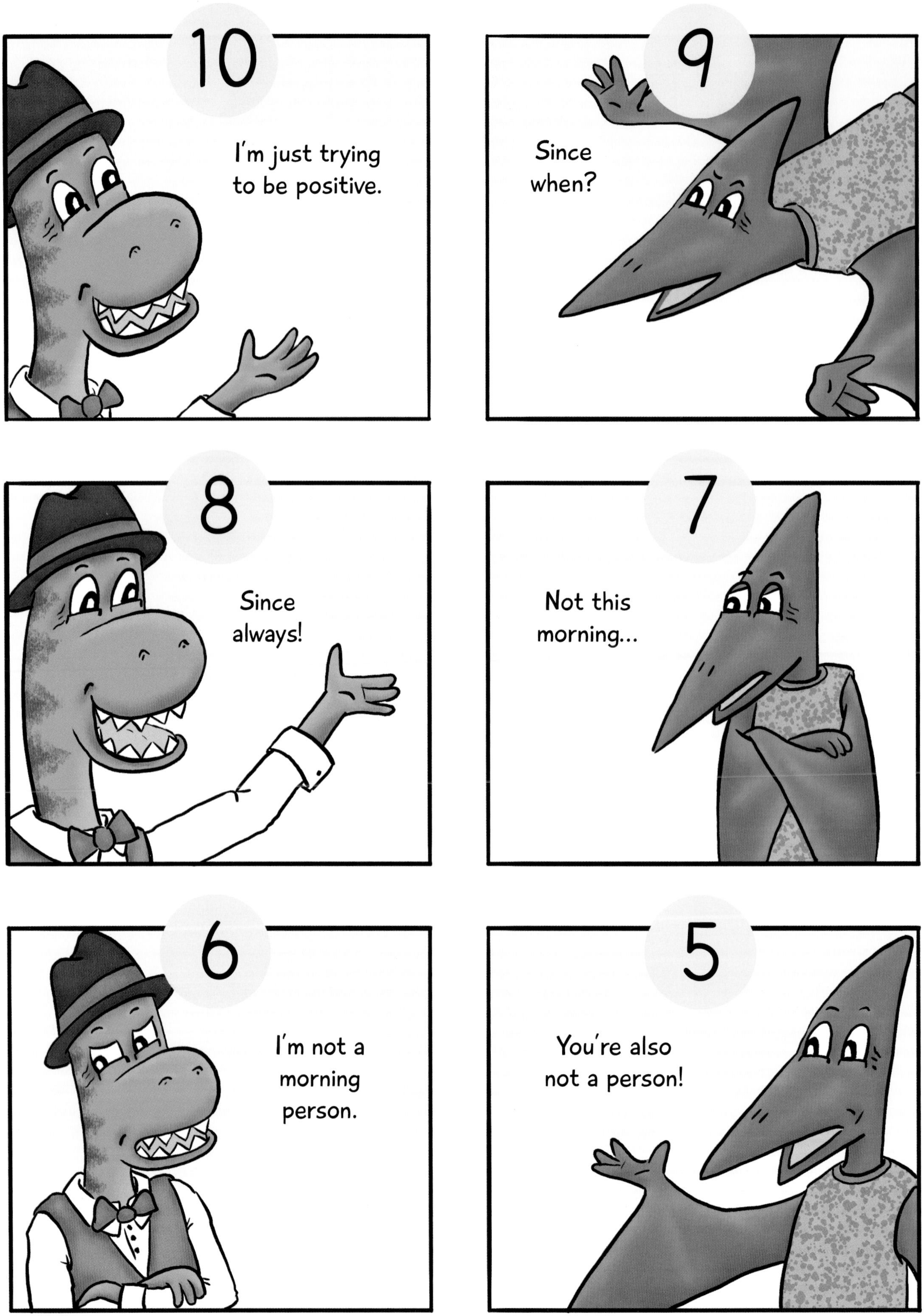
10
I'm just trying to be positive.
9
Since when?
8
Since always!
7
Not this morning...
6
I'm not a morning person.
5
You're also not a person!

4
Speaking of people, the kid's peeking!
3
NO PEEKING!
2
Scramble
Scramble
Scramble
1
Flap
Flap
Flap
Now say:
Ready or not, here I come!

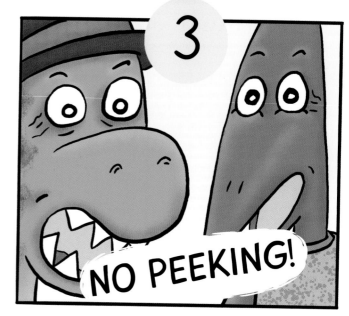

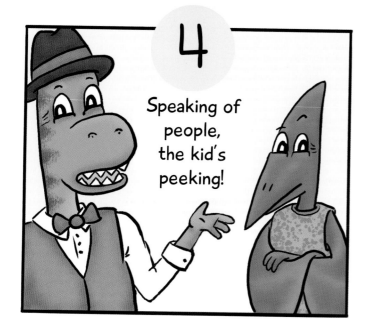

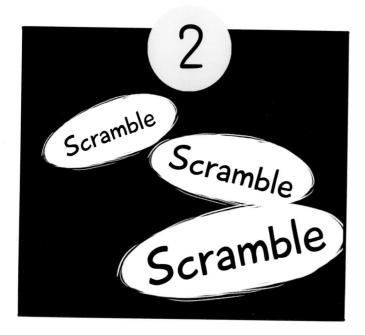

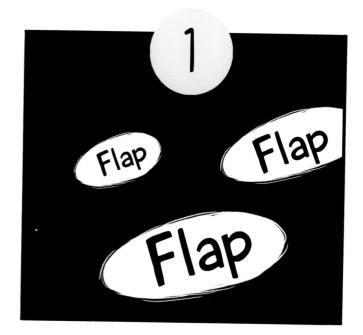

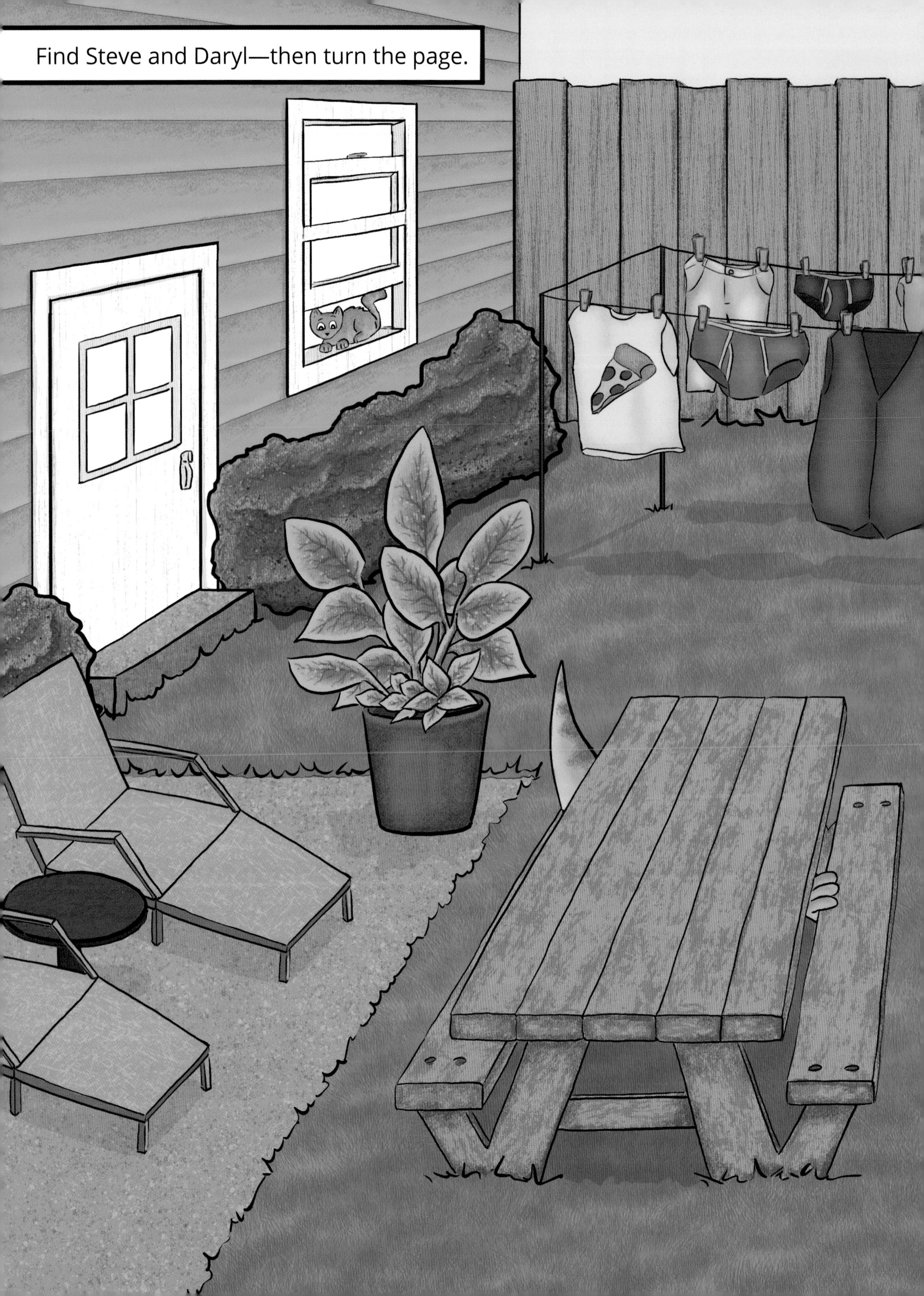
Find Steve and Daryl—then turn the page.

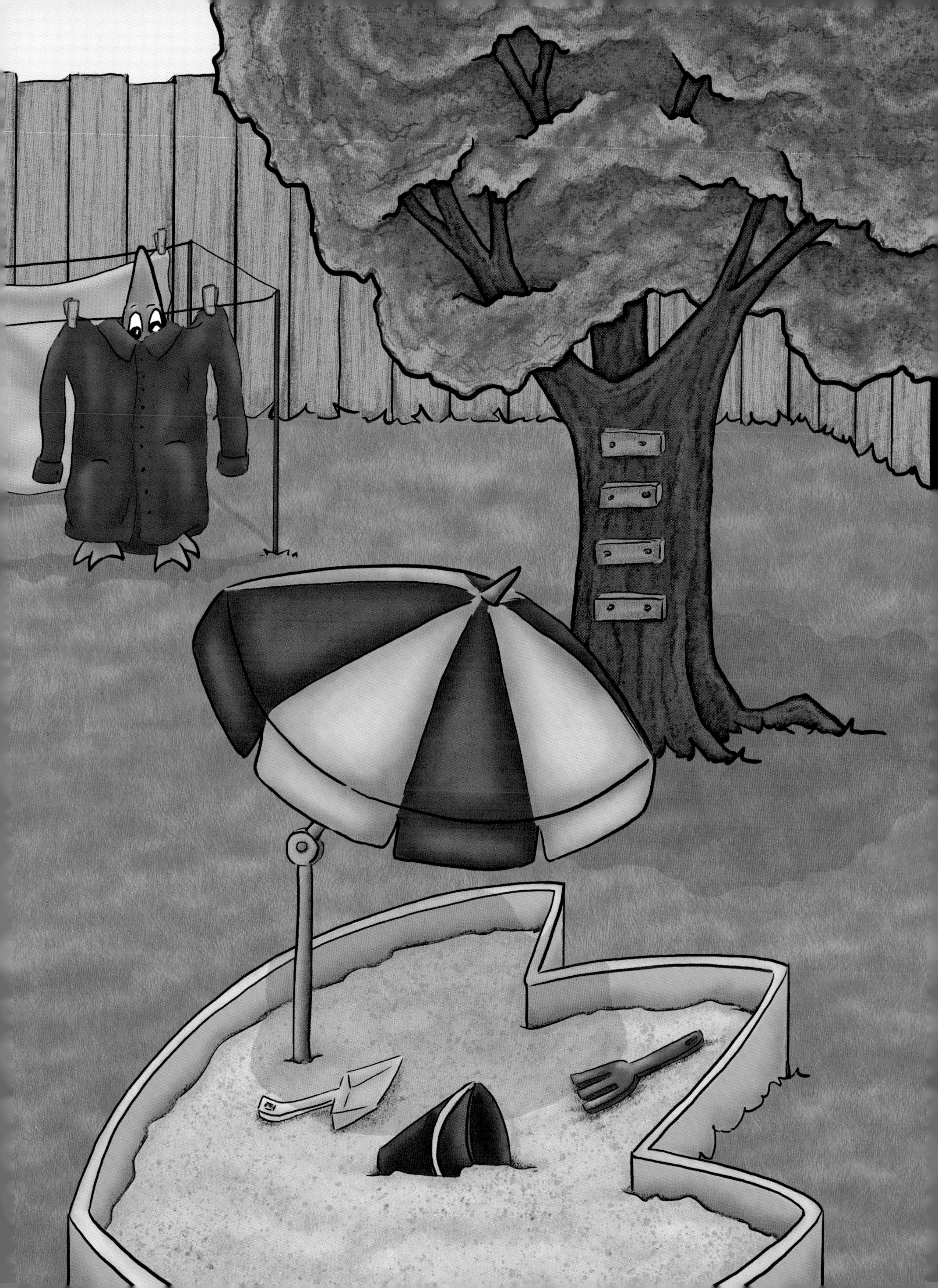

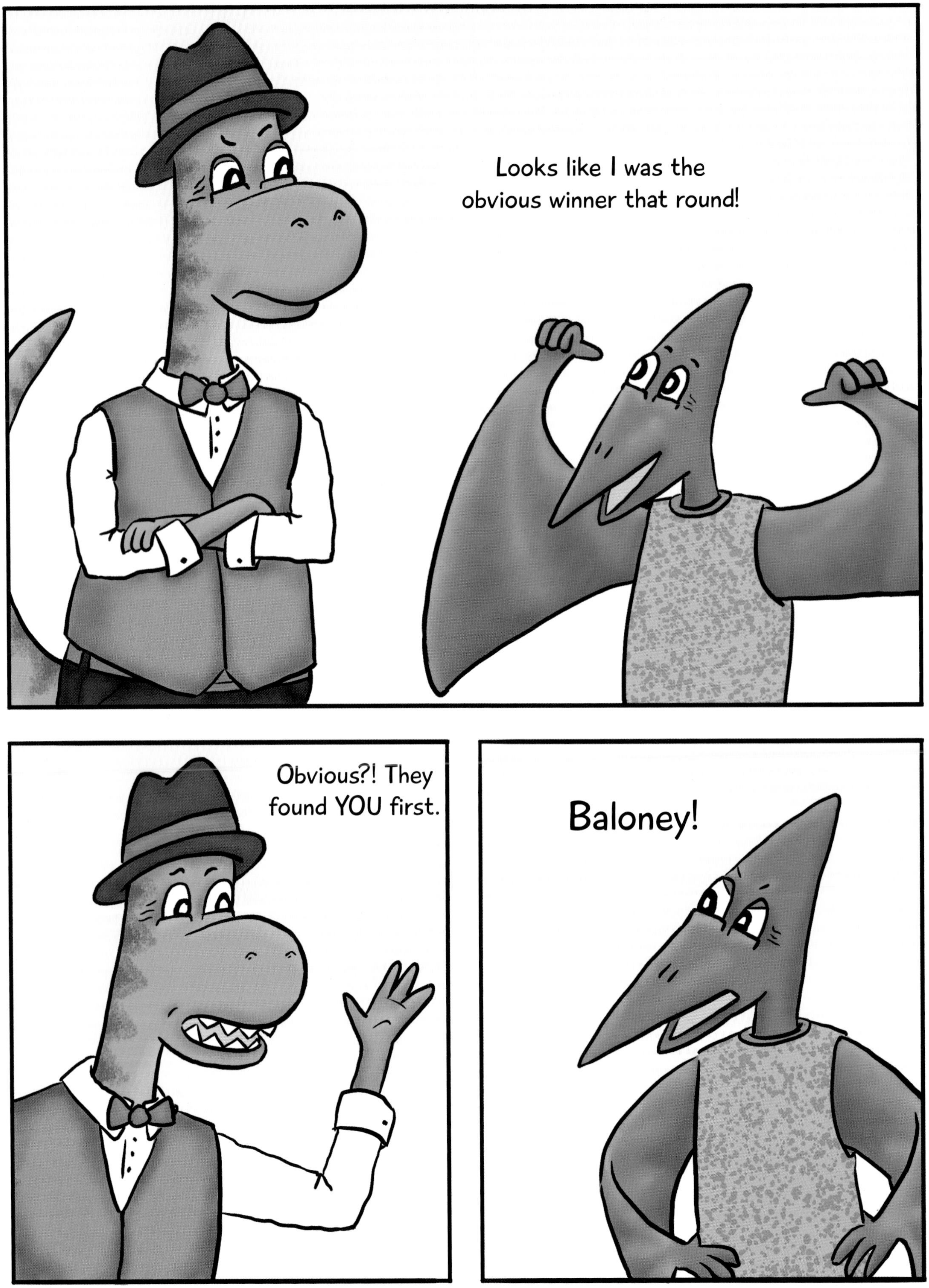
Looks like I was the obvious winner that round!
Obvious?! They found YOU first.
Baloney!

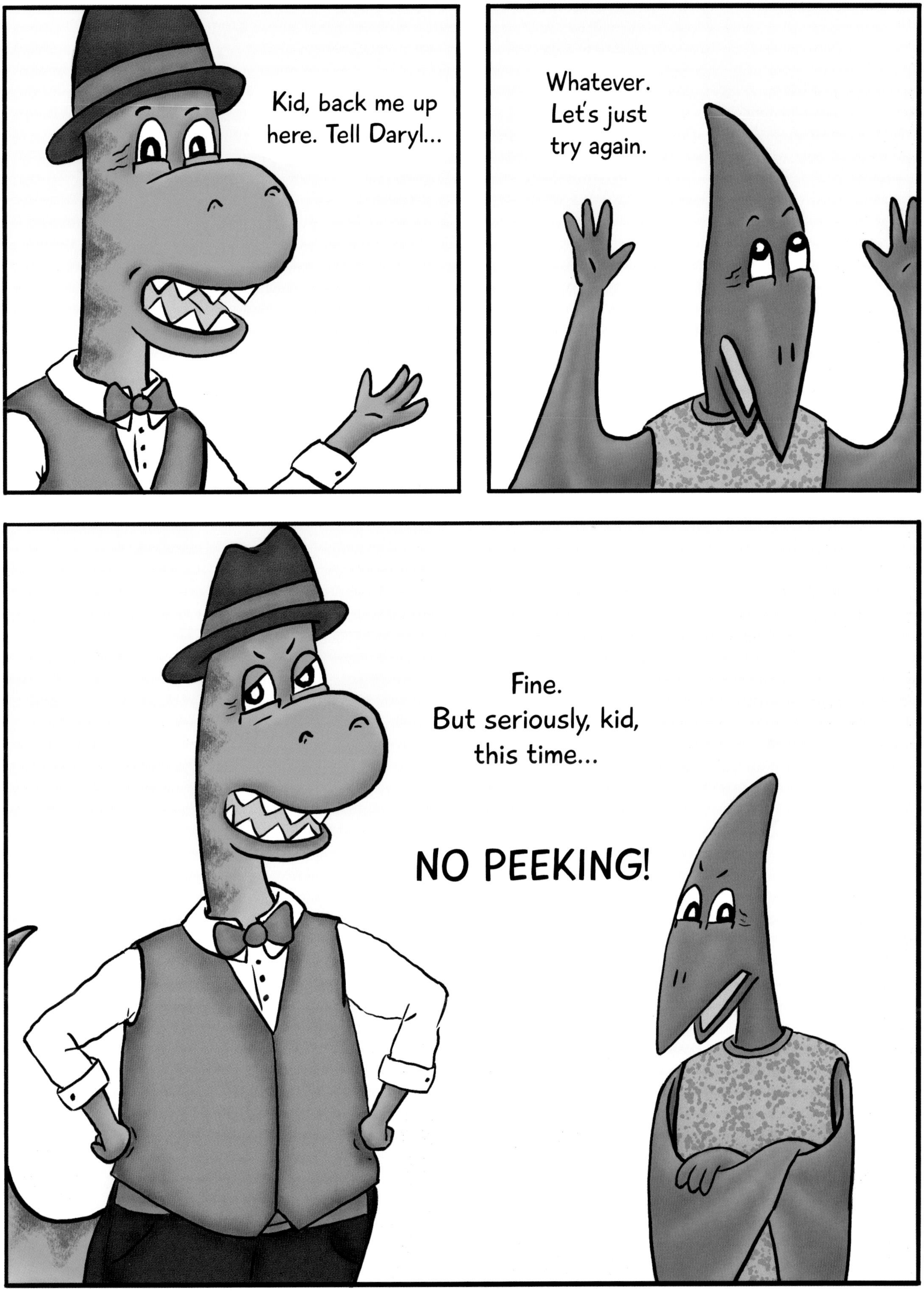
Kid, back me up here. Tell Daryl...
Whatever. Let's just try again.
Fine. But seriously, kid, this time...
NO PEEKING!

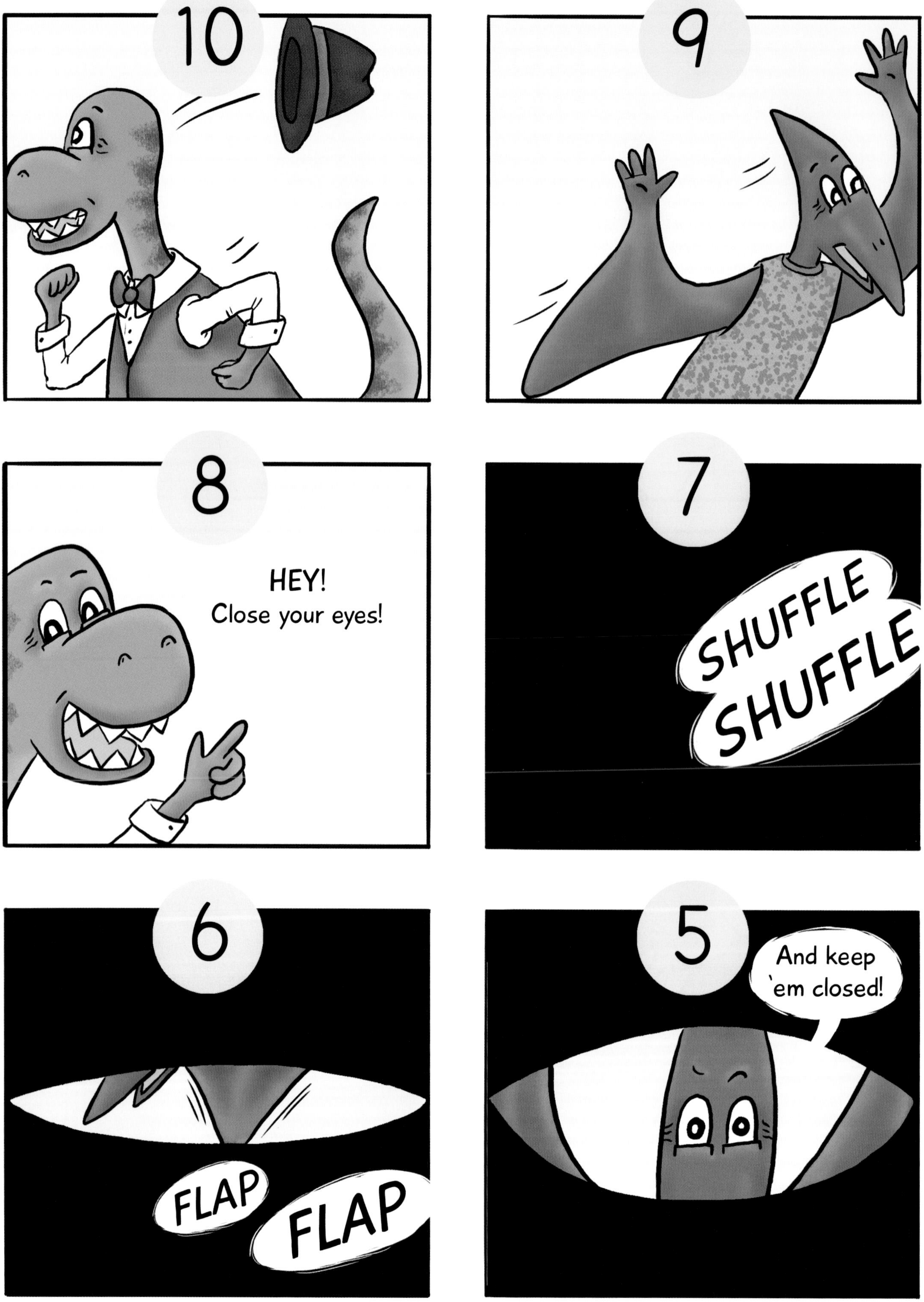
10
9
8
HEY!
Close your eyes!
7
SHUFFLE
SHUFFLE
6
FLAP
FLAP
5
And keep
`em closed!

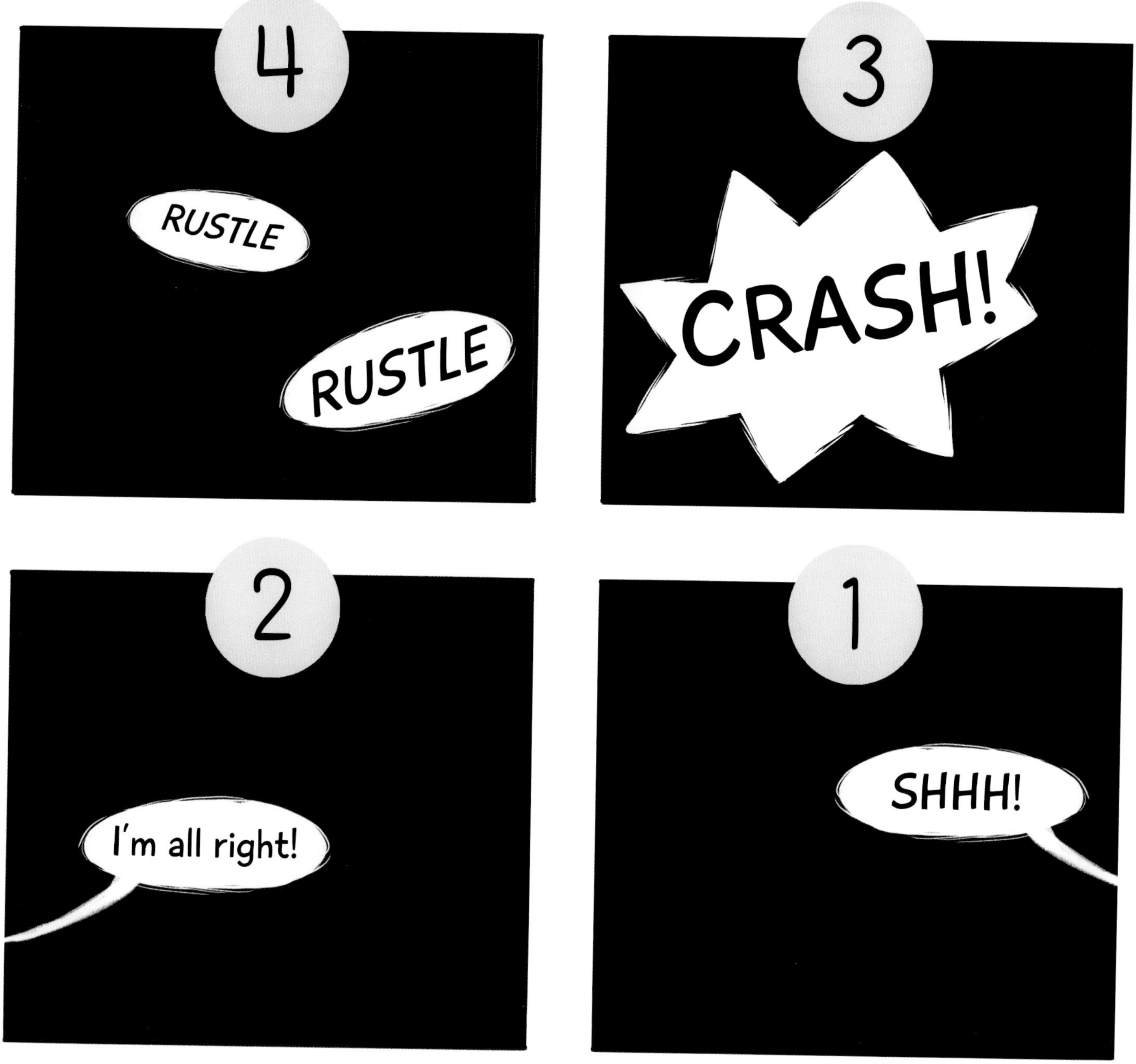
4
RUSTLE
RUSTLE
3
CRASH!
2
I'm all right!
1
SHHH!

That's your cue:

Ready or not, here I come!

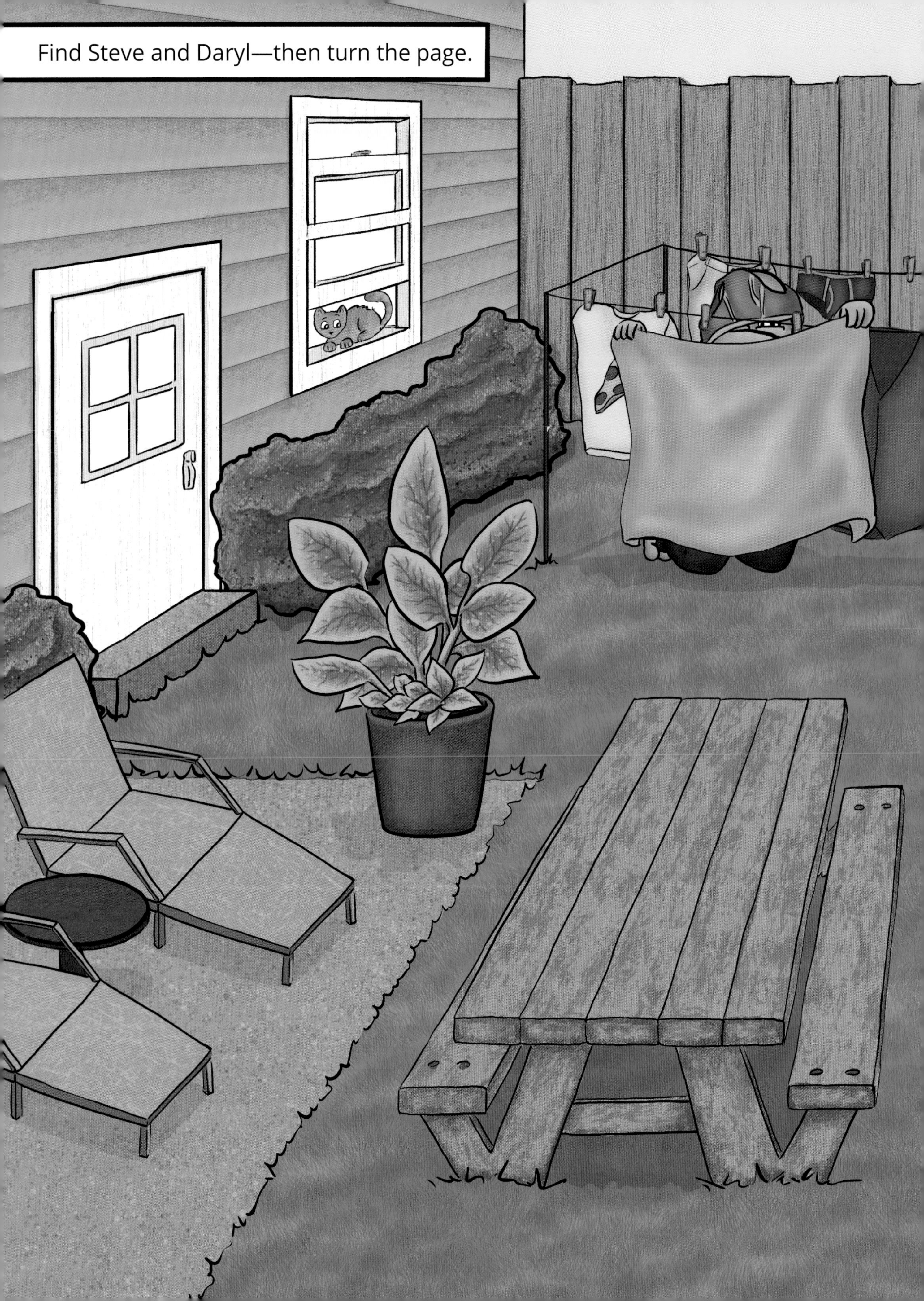
Find Steve and Daryl—then turn the page.

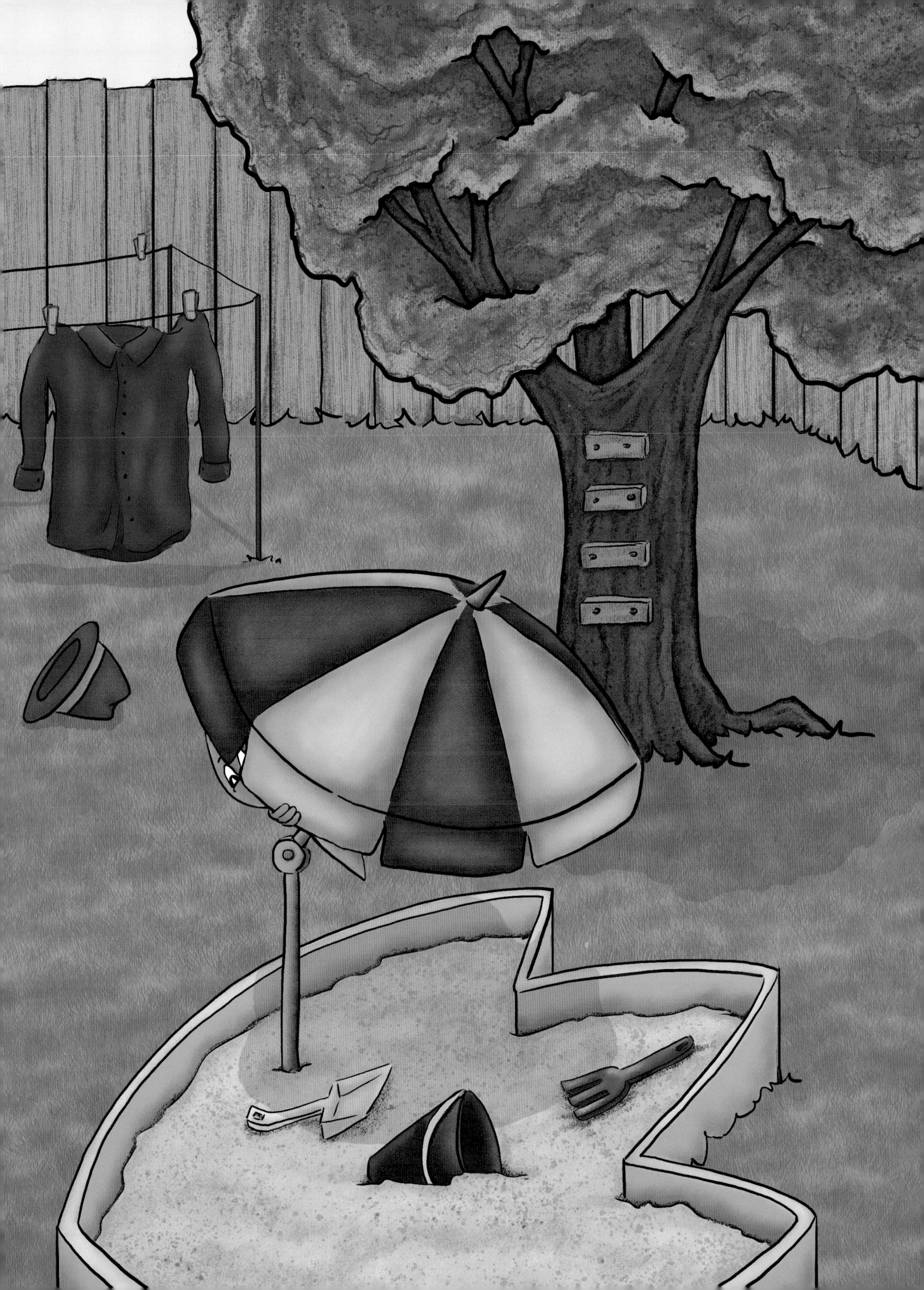

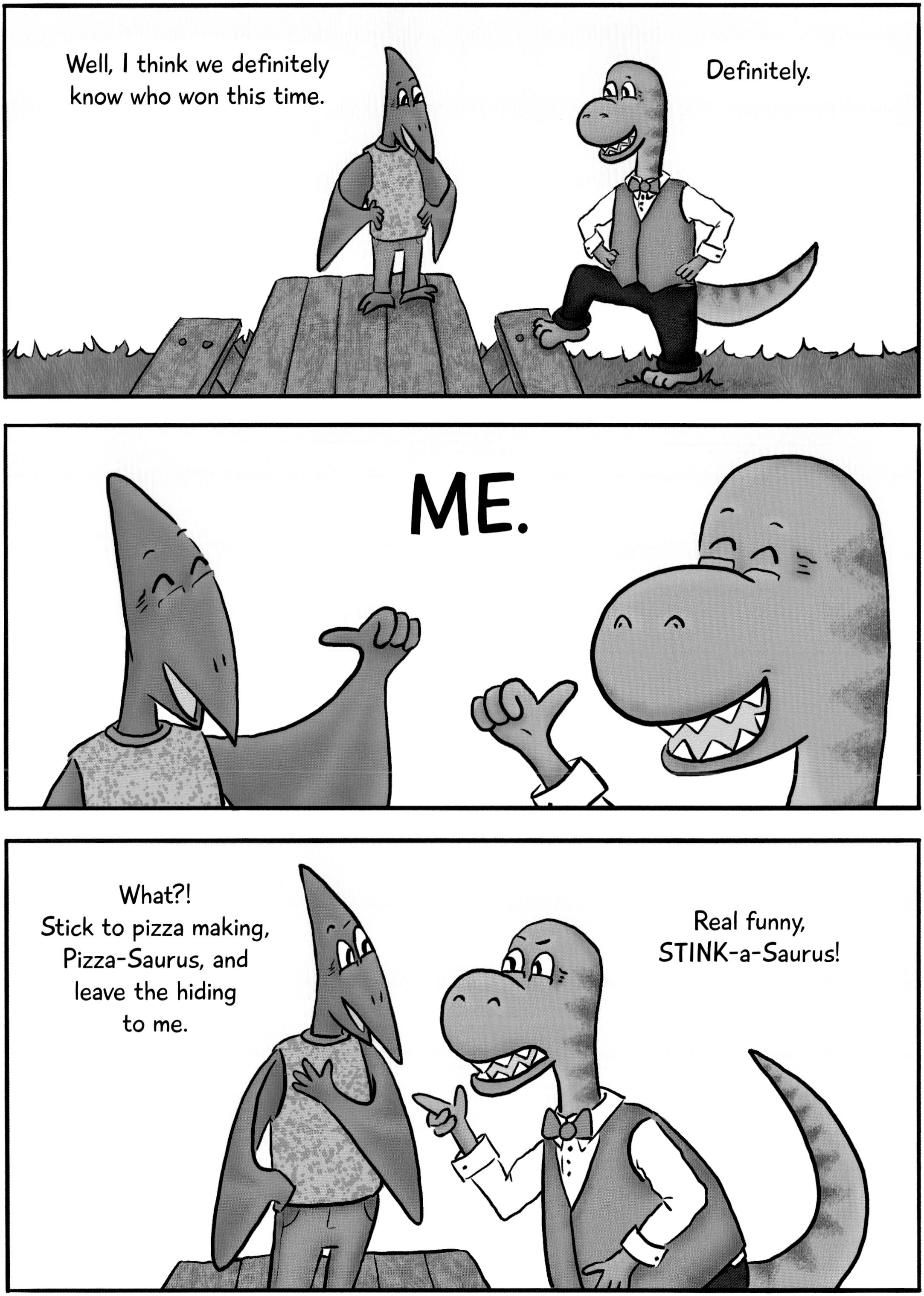
Well, I think we definitely know who won this time.
Definitely.
ME.
What?! Stick to pizza making, Pizza-Saurus, and leave the hiding to me.
Real funny, STINK-a-Saurus!

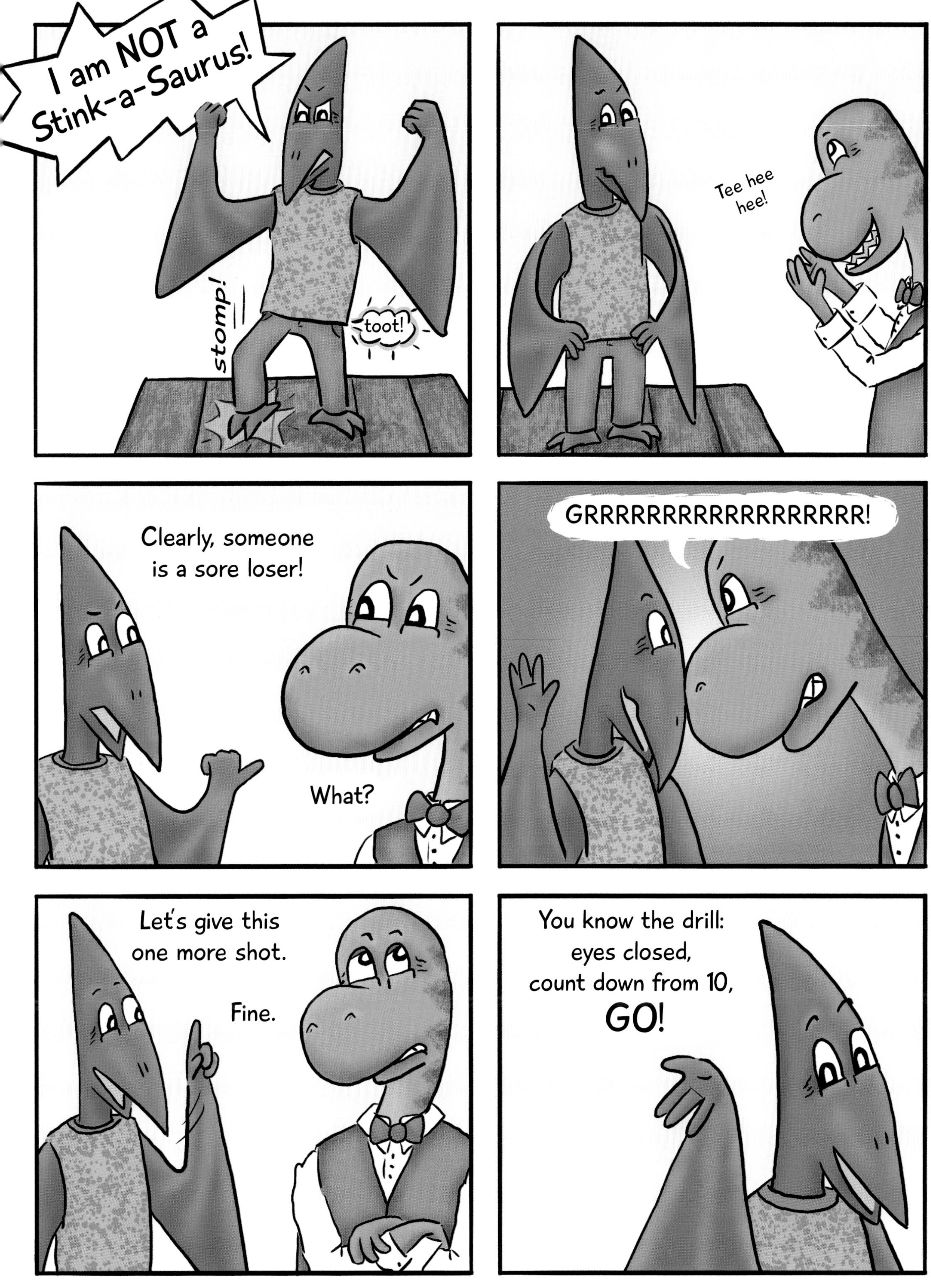
I am NOT a Stink-a-Saurus!
stomp!
toot!
Tee hee hee!
Clearly, someone is a sore loser!
What?
GRRRRRRRRRRRRRRRRRR!
Let's give this one more shot.
Fine.
You know the drill: eyes closed, count down from 10, GO!

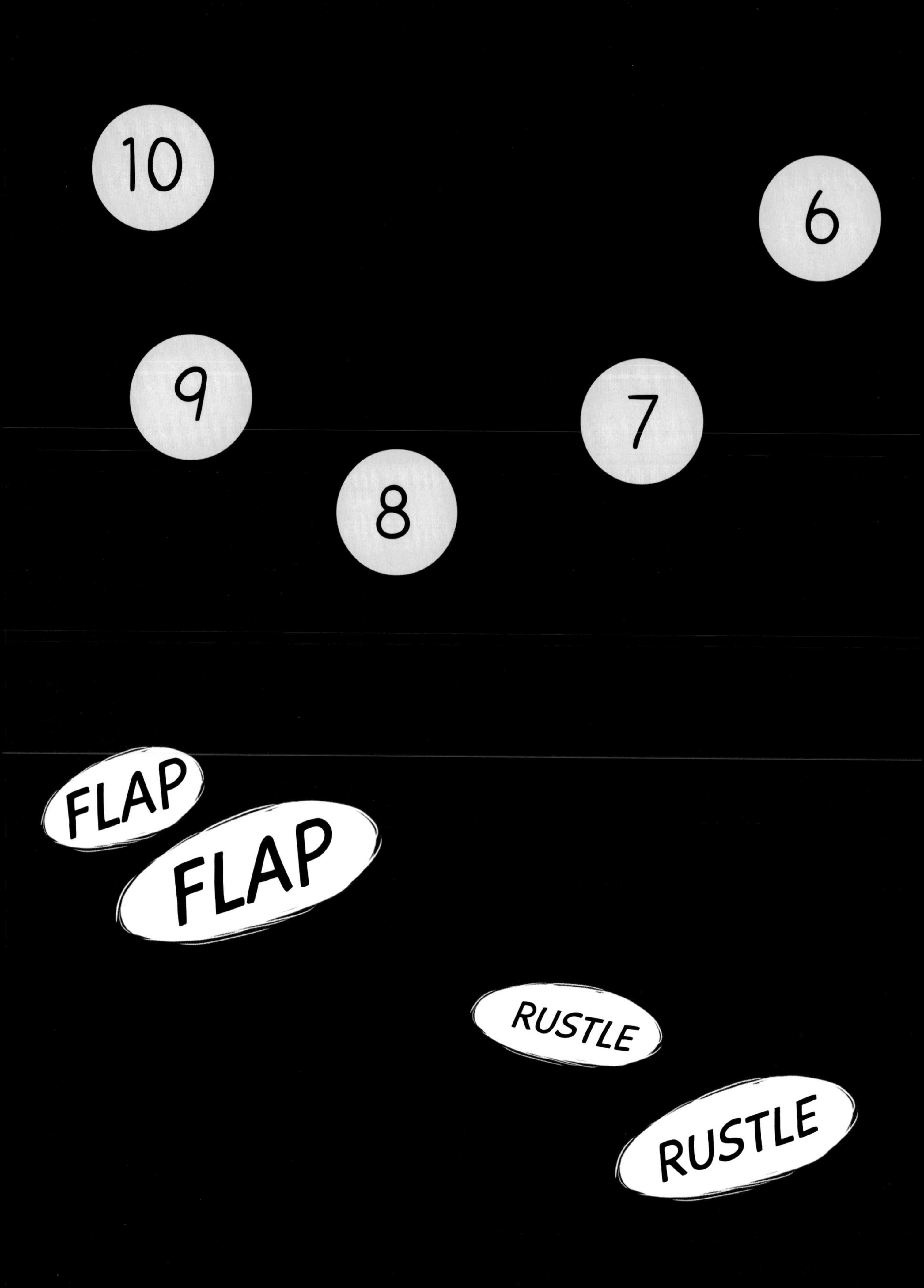
10
9
8
7
6
FLAP
FLAP
RUSTLE
RUSTLE

5

4

THUD!

3

CRUNCH

THUMP

2

1

Ready or not,
here I come!

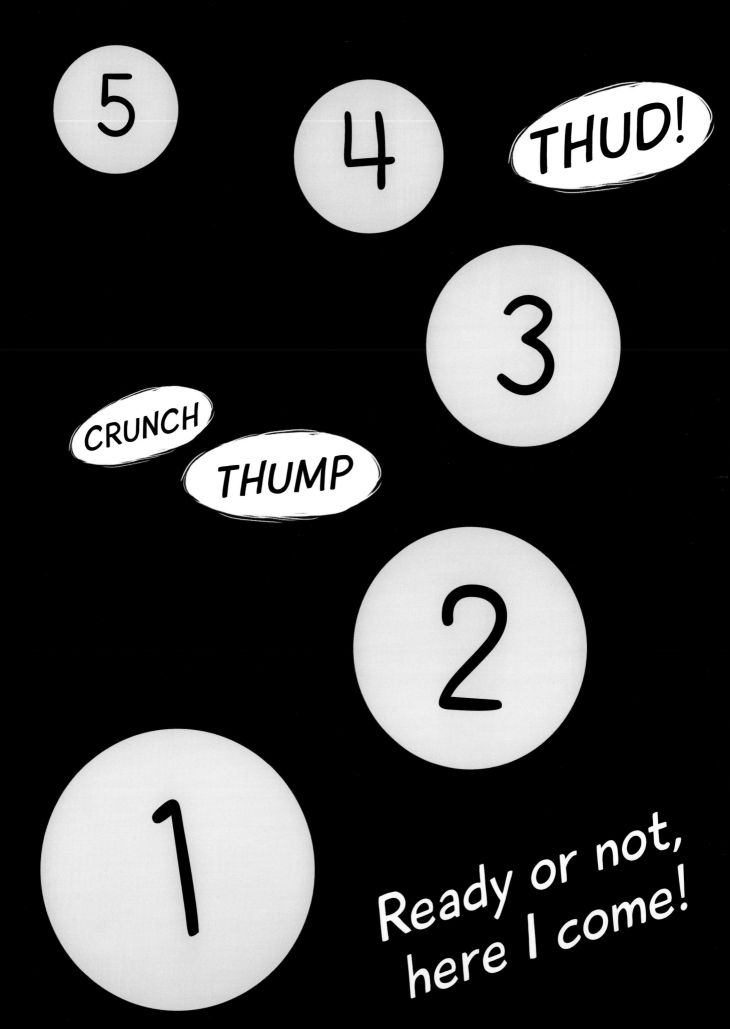

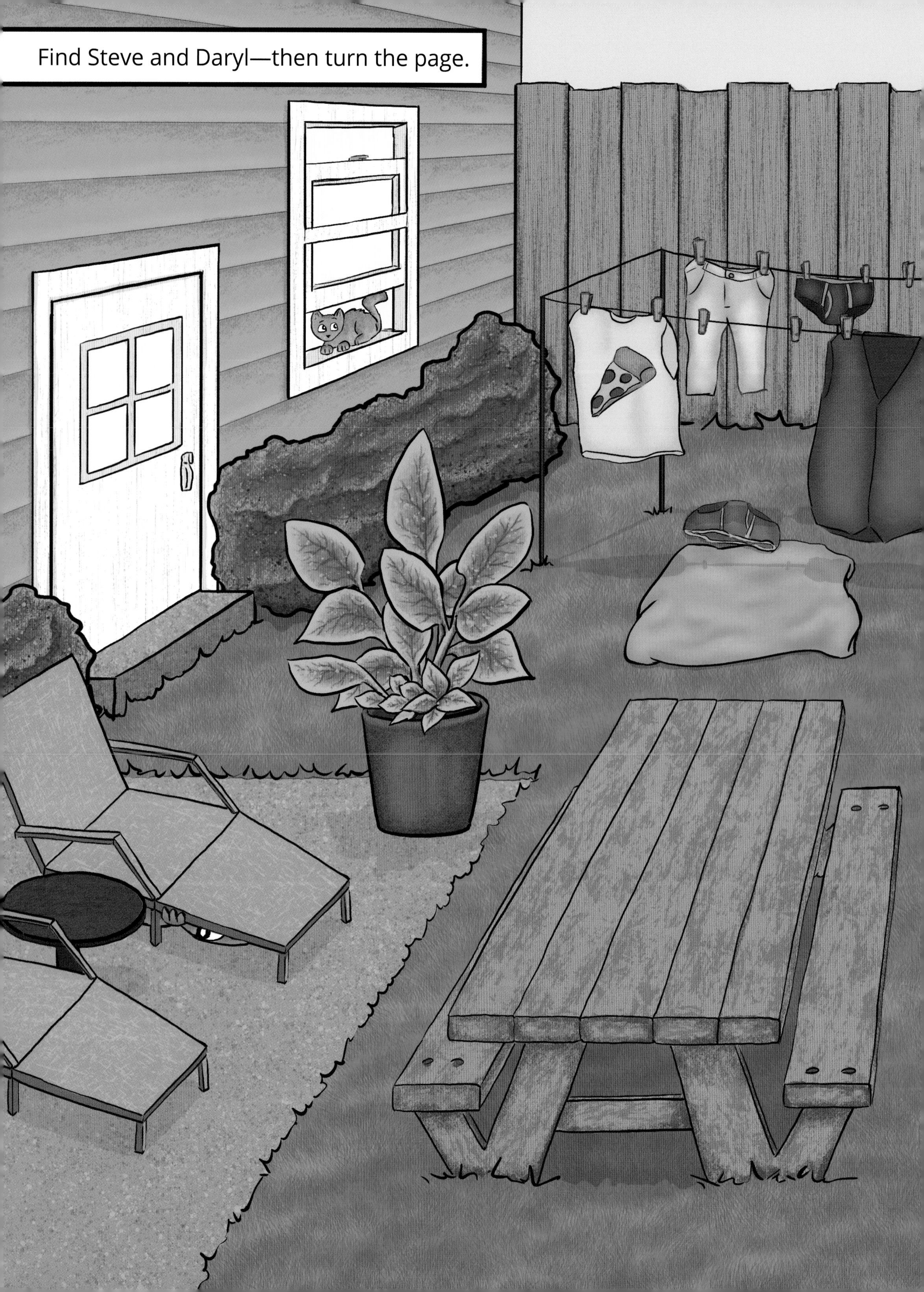
Find Steve and Daryl—then turn the page.

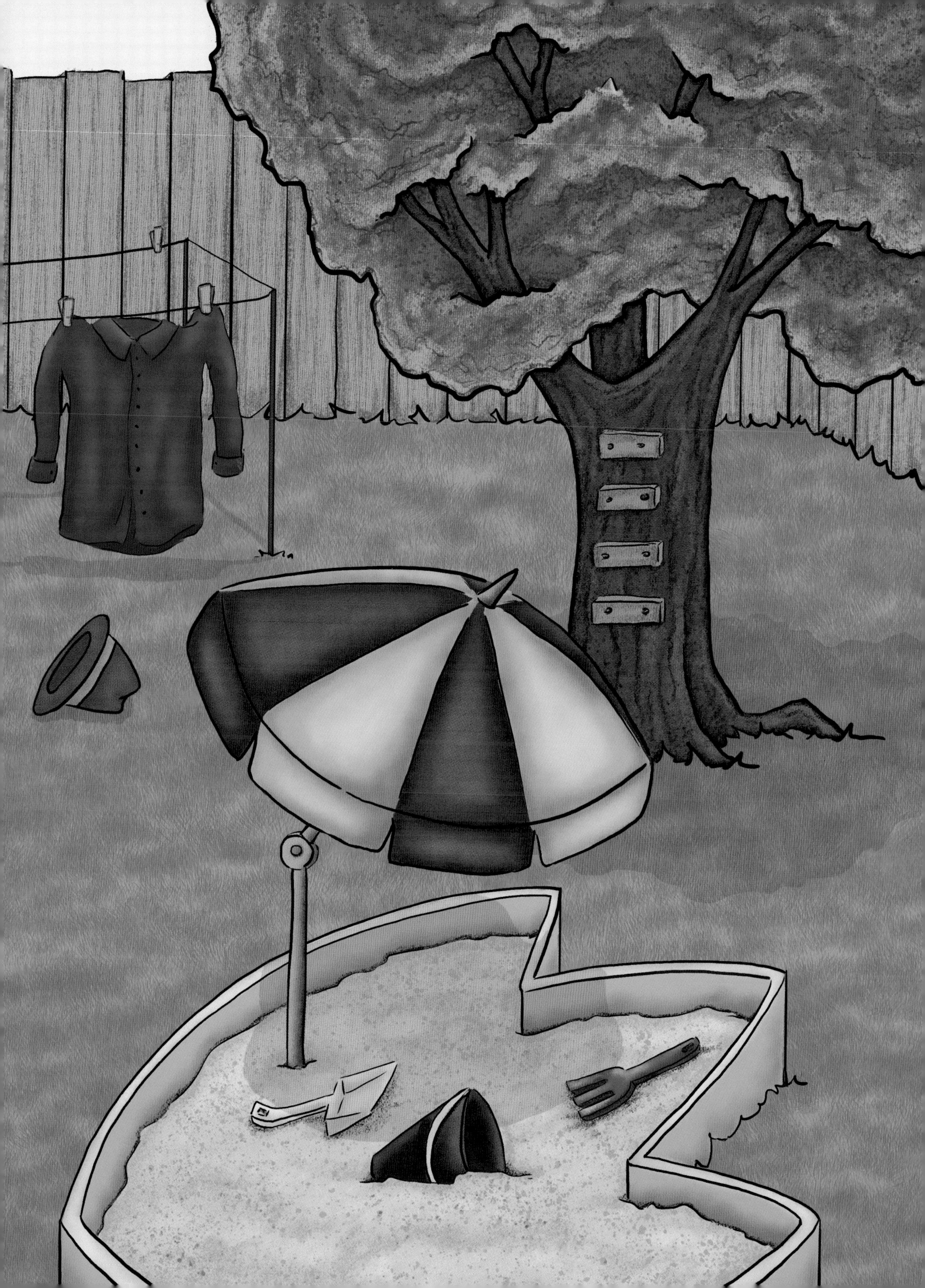

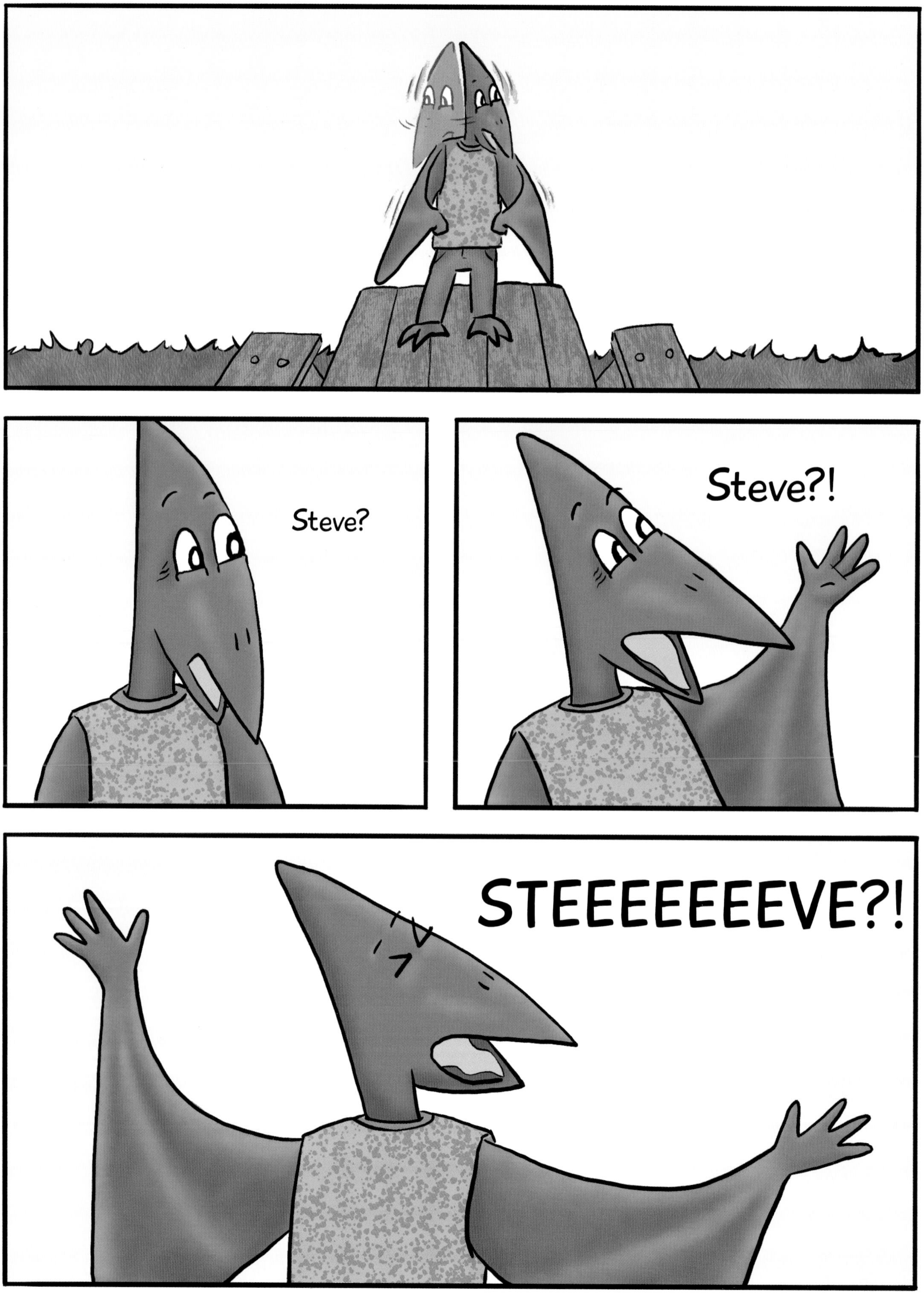
Steve?
Steve?!
STEEEEEEEEVE?!

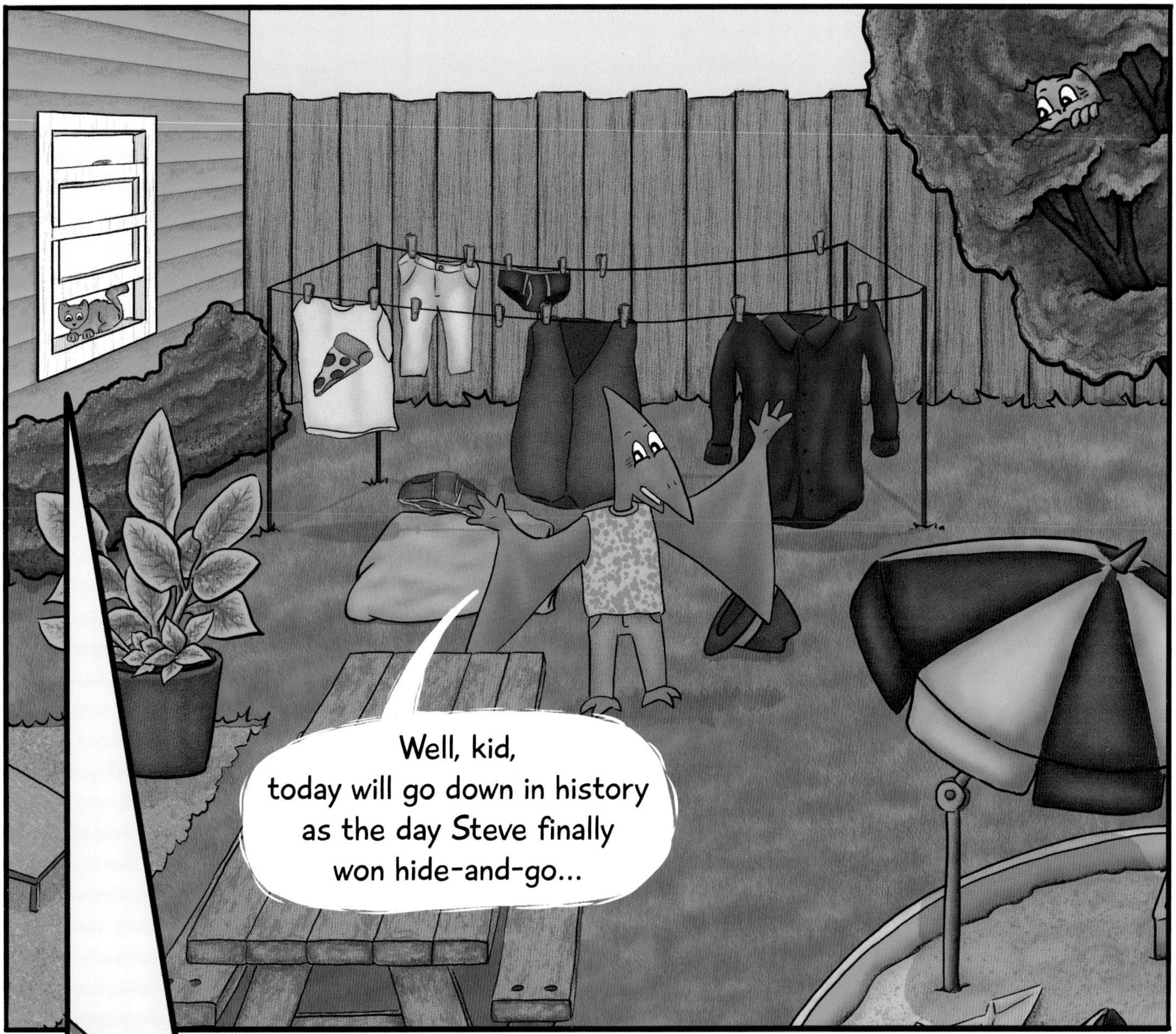
Well, kid,
today will go down in history
as the day Steve finally
won hide-and-go...

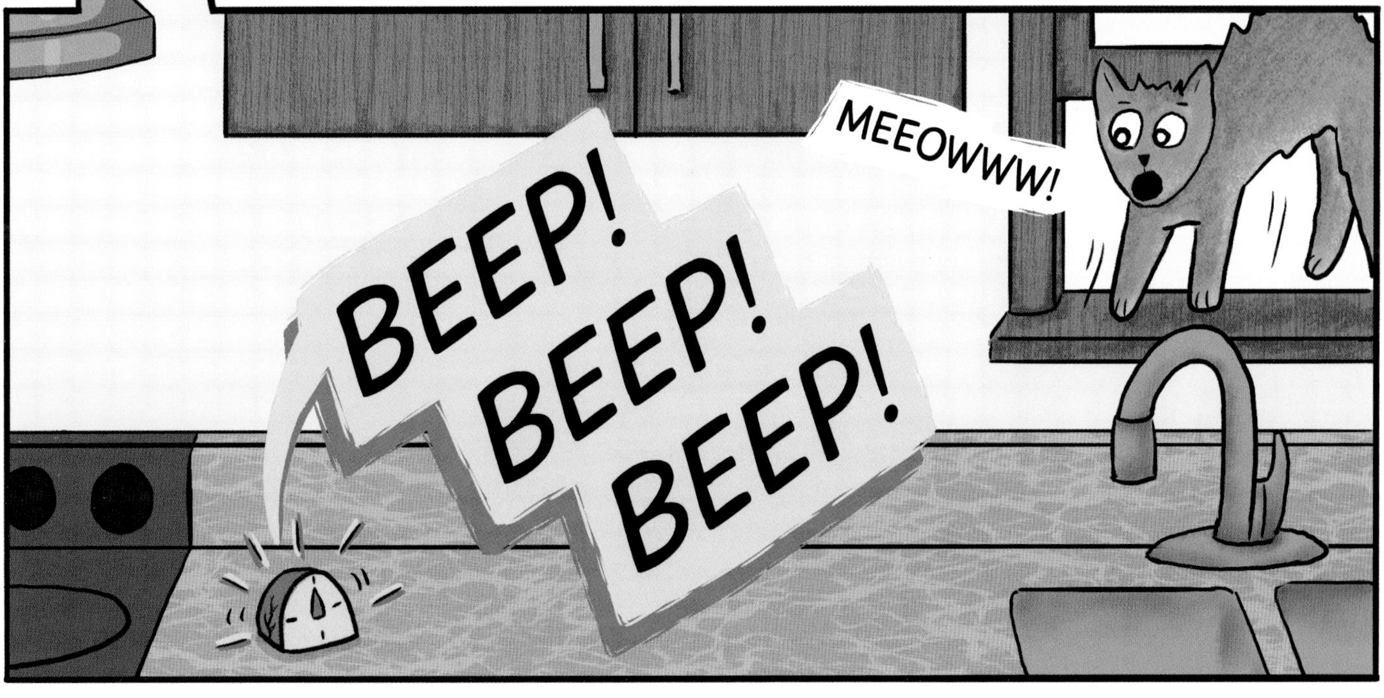
MEEOWWW!
BEEP! BEEP! BEEP!

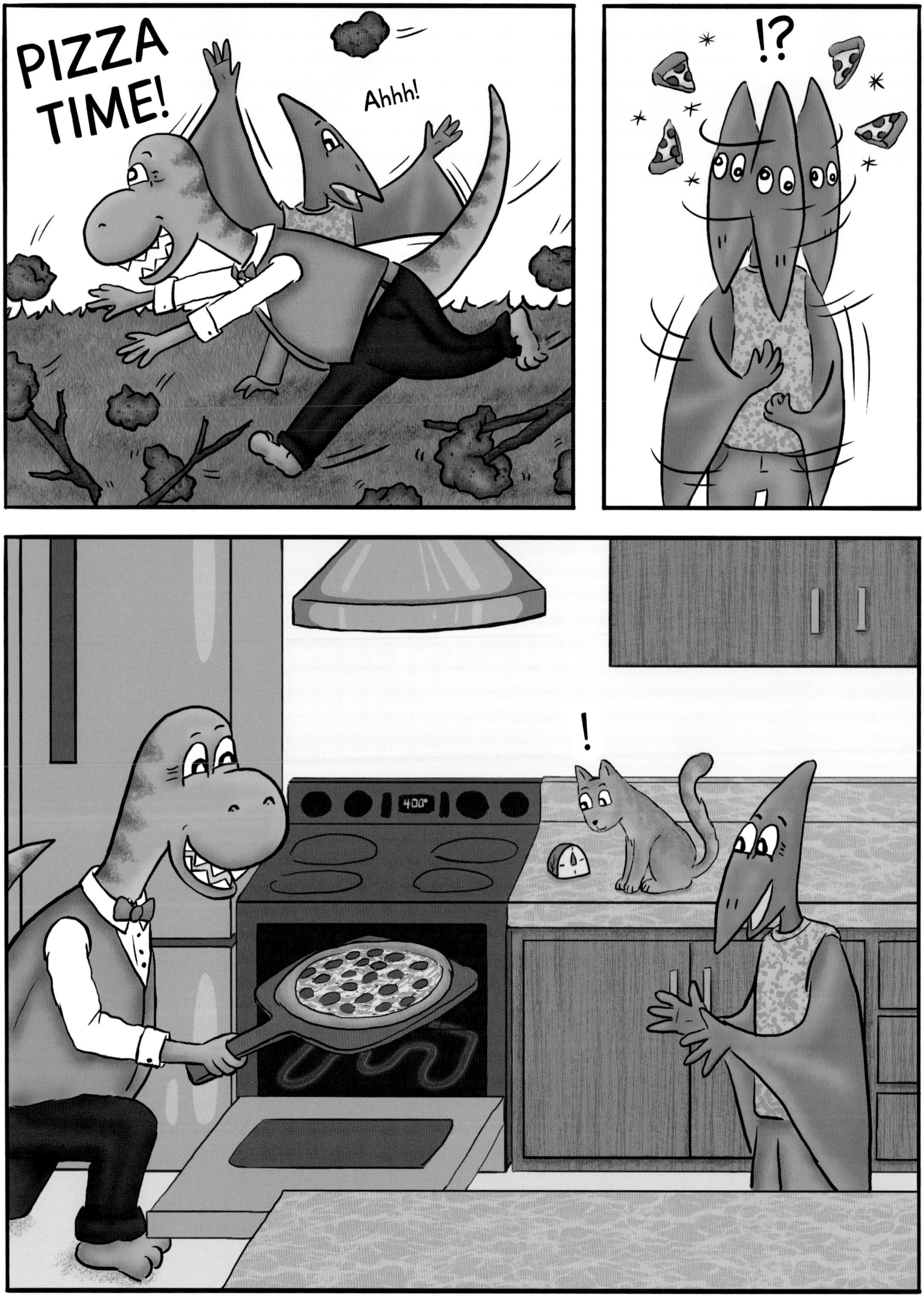
PIZZA TIME!
Ahhh!
!?
400°
!

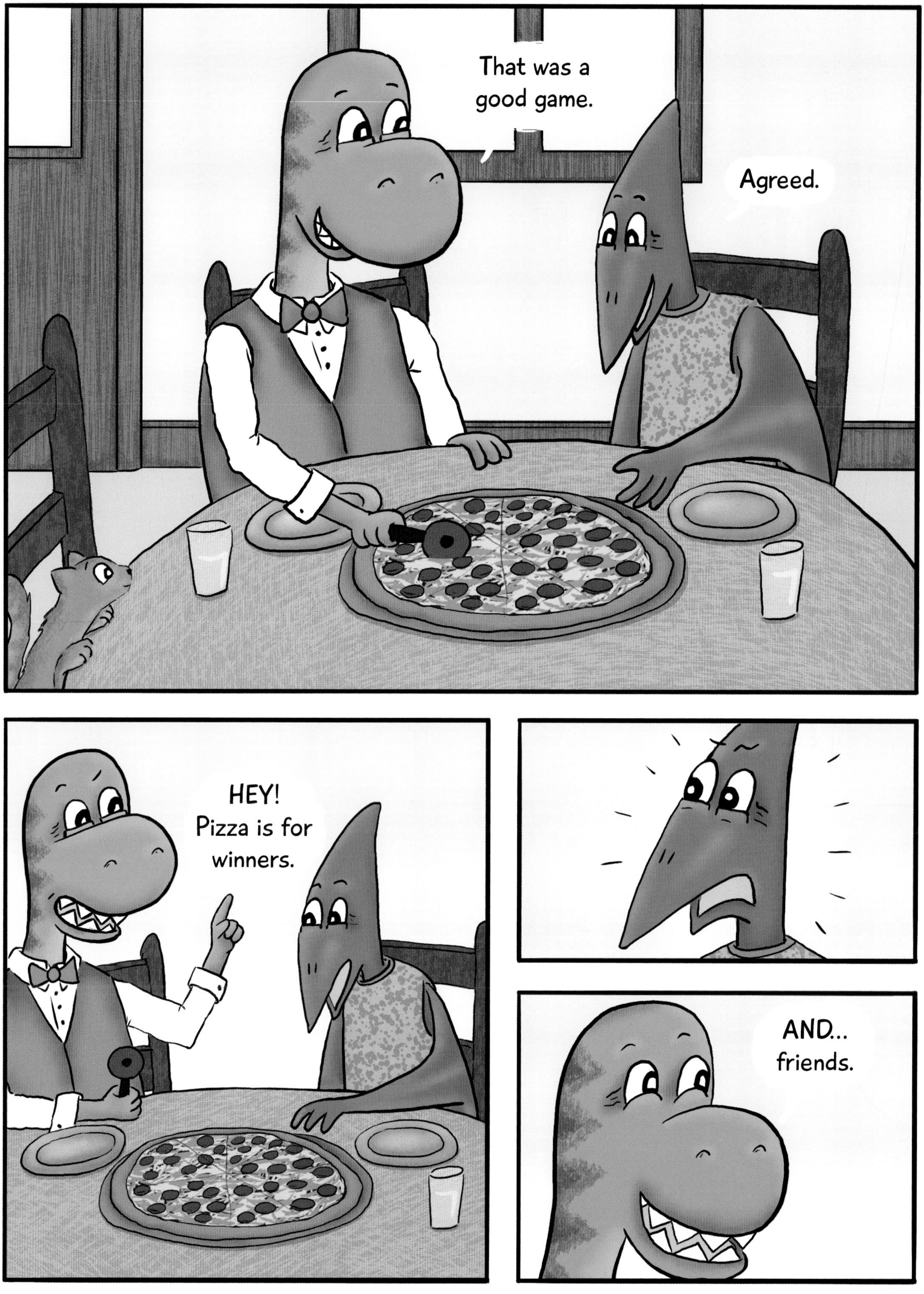
That was a good game.
Agreed.
HEY! Pizza is for winners.
AND... friends.

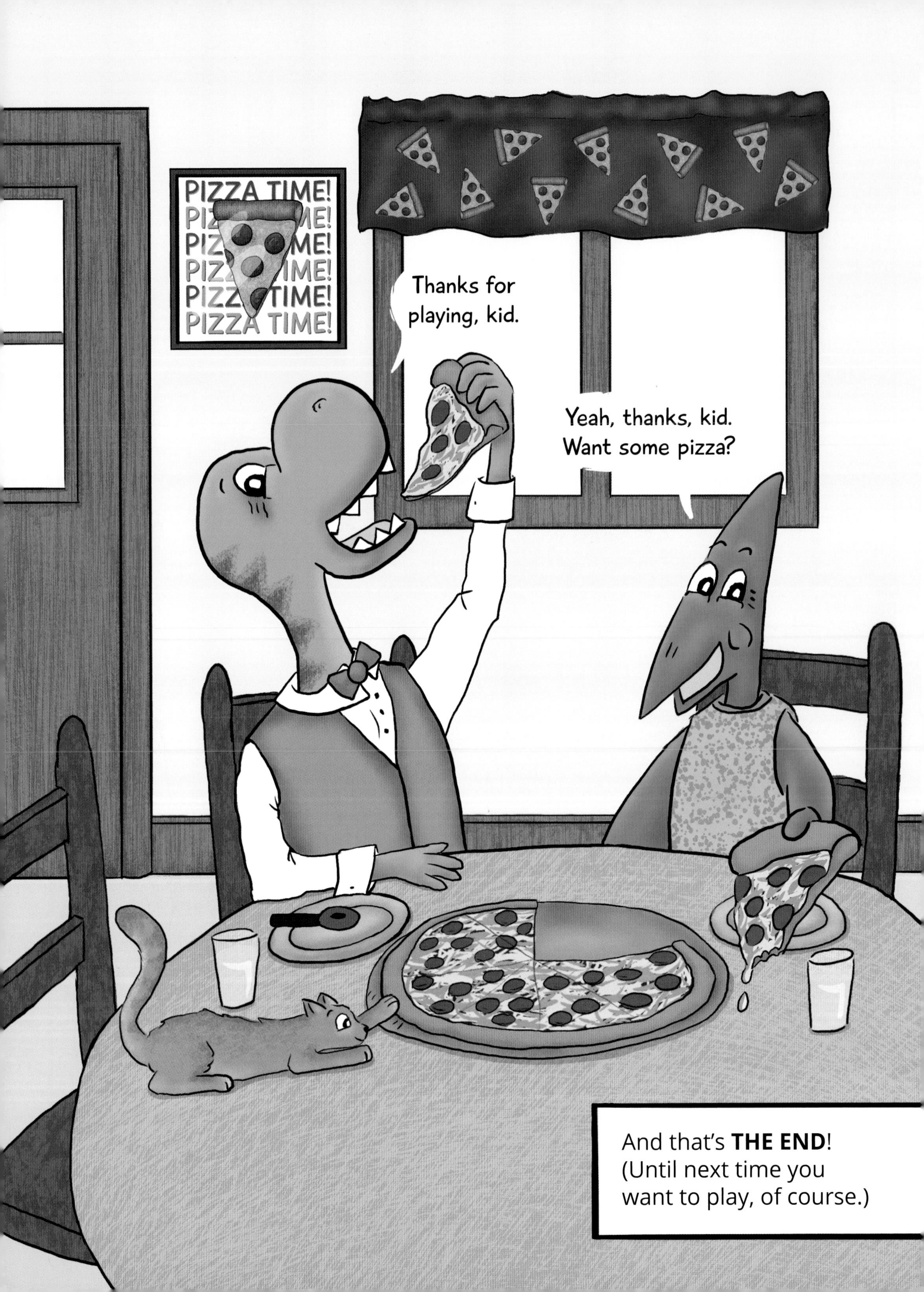
PIZZA TIME!
Thanks for playing, kid.
Yeah, thanks, kid. Want some pizza?
And that's **THE END**! (Until next time you want to play, of course.)

To Mom & Dad,
for everything...
and all the pizza.
~SMR

KWiL Publishing, LLC
Milwaukee, Wisconsin, USA
kwilpublishing.com

Publisher's Cataloging-in-Publication Data

Names: Roloff, Sheri, author illustrator.
Title: Hide and go seek-a-saurus / Sheri Roloff.
Description: Milwaukee, WI: KWiL Publishing, 2018.
Summary: Two dinosaurs invite the reader to play hide-and-go-seek.
Identifiers: ISBN 978-0-9991437-1-1 | LCCN 2017959845
Subjects: LCSH Dinosaurs—Juvenile fiction. | Hide-and-seek—Juvenile fiction.
BISAC JUVENILE FICTION / Animals / Dinosaurs & Prehistoric Creatures.
JUVENILE FICTION / Sports & Recreation / Games.
Classification: LCC PZ7.R654 Hi 2018 | DDC [E]—dc23

Book design by Sheri Roloff
Primary typeface is Playtime with Hot Toddies
Narrator typeface is Open Sans
Title typeface is Bourton Hand
Numbers typeface is SF Cartoonist Hand SC

The illustrations in this book were created digitally.

Printed in Stevens Point, Wisconsin, USA

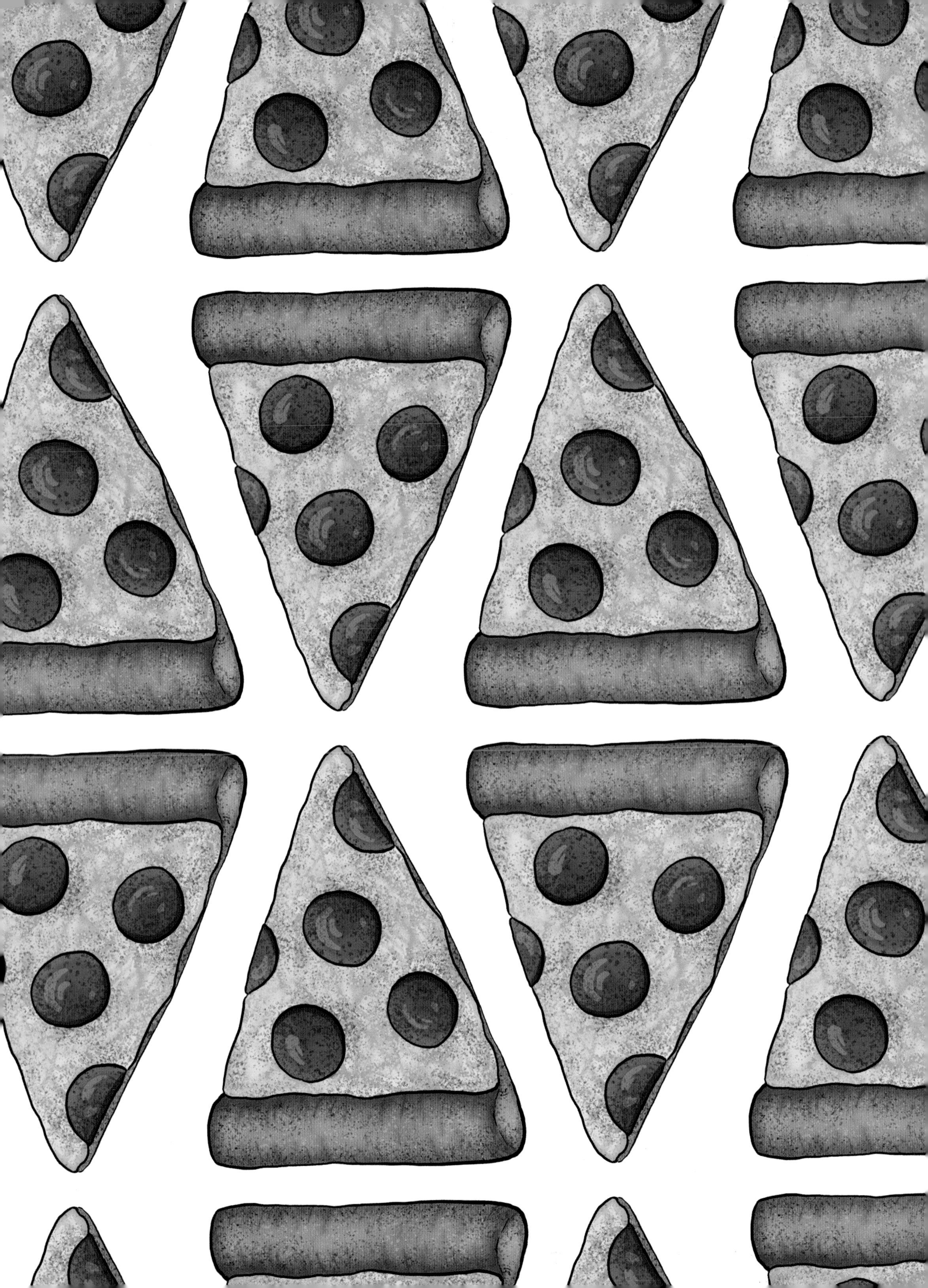